The Darkening Season
A collection of poetry, fiction and memoirs

Otley Writers

CHEVIN
Manuscripts

Copyright © The copyright remains with the individual authors.

The right to be identified as authors of these works has been asserted by them in accordance with the Copyright, Designs and Patents Act 1988.

All rights reserved. No part of this publication may be reproduced, stored in a retrieval system, or transmitted in any form or by means, electronic, mechanical, photocopying, recording, or otherwise, without the prior permission of the author.

A CIP catalogue record for this title is available from the British Library.

ISBN – 13 : 978 - 1976095580

Introduction

What a brilliant year our writing group is having!

We meet every Friday morning to share our work and make so much noise and laugh so much that it probably should be illegal. The fact that we are in the Judges' Robing Room of the old Otley Courthouse makes the fun we are having even more enjoyably naughty.

Picture a room with twelve or so writers, for each of whom the word 'quirky' was probably invented, all sitting around a table. At their head, probably giggling helplessly, I sit, The King of Quirkiness, attempting to steer the group, introducing topics, exercises and continually astounded at the quality of writing produced. Sometimes I have to call for order, and sometimes I succeed.

There is an energy in this amazing group which has meant that many of them have been published over the last few years, won competitions and performed their work successfully. From this energy came their first joint anthology 'The Pulse of Everything' earlier this year, and this is their second collection which celebrates the shortening of days and the drawing in of nights, perhaps the time to make a cuppa, reach for those biscuits and settle down to read this fabulous collections of poems and stories.

I am in awe of their talent, and proud to be of their number,

James Nash,

October 2017

Contents

Alex L Williams ………………………………….. 1

Martin P Fuller ……………………………….. 7

Gearr …………………………………………….. 23

Jo Campbell ……………………………………... 35

Laura Driver …………………………………….43

Polly Smith ……………………………………… 53

Saille …………………………………………….59

Alyson Faye ……………………………………81

James Nash ……………………………………93

John Ellis ……………………………………….. 99

Cynthia Richardson ……………………………125

Peter Dawson ………………………………...135

Pauline Harrowell ……………………………...139

Sandy Wilson …………………………………...143

The Darkening Season

Alex L Williams

Many years ago, I was standing in my front garden talking to my neighbour. As we chatted we saw a middle-aged man in a tutu with a large knitted teapot on his head running down the road. I looked at my neighbour ready to pass judgement on the spectacle, but he just smiled and said, 'Why not?' in his transatlantic accent.

This has stayed with me over the years and I often think 'why not?' when I see unusual behaviour.

The 'why not?' philosophy has affected my writing too. Could a shadow think for itself? Could a mushroom be a ghost? Could a man live inside a shell? The answer to all these questions has been a resounding 'why not?'

I am currently working on a flash fiction collection of quirky stories and run a children's book business called 'Half Man Half Octopus.' Find out more at halfmanhalfoctopus.co.uk

The Darkening Season

Halloween Mushroom

I always went for a woodland walk on October 31st, it was my Halloween tradition. This year the sky was bright and clear and the leaves were turning yellow. I sat on the trunk of a fallen tree in the woods for a rest and noticed a hoard of small grey mushrooms growing on the damp bark surface.

I examined them in more detail and that was when I saw it. One of the mushrooms had a tiny face, the features resembling those of an old man with a pronounced nose. I gasped in shock then decided it must be a trick of the light so I peered more closely.

'What are you staring at?' asked the mushroom. I stood up and looked around, there was no one in sight so I crouched down in front of the talking fungus.

'Hello?' I said. I felt for my iPhone in my pocket. I knew I had to get a video of this.

'What are you doing?' The fungus asked anxiously.

'I'm just having a sit down before I carry on with my walk. How about you?'

The Darkening Season

'Well I may as well tell you.... you see, it is indeed the case that all mushrooms are ghosts, however the faces can't usually be seen.

'So how come I can see yours?' I slipped the phone out of my pocket.

'Something's gone wrong. I don't know why, perhaps it's because it's Halloween,' it said, its small grey eyebrows furrowing slightly. I held up my phone ready to film. 'Don't take a photo!' the mushroom shouted. 'Living humans can't know about this.... It would ruin the flow of everything.'

'Just one. I won't show anyone.' I knew I had the power, I mean mushrooms didn't even have legs or arms. The little mushroom ghost couldn't stop me filming. This was going to be a YouTube sensation.

Suddenly all the mushrooms started waking up, quivering and rustling, faces appearing on each of them. The one with the old man's face started rocking more violently. My hands started trembling and I dropped my phone.

'I did warn you,' he whispered.

The mushrooms got bigger and bigger. Then they let out thousands of tiny spores, spraying them out at an alarming speed.

I stood up, ready to run but it was too late. I was breathing in the strange dust. I fell to the floor and passed out.

When I woke up I felt different. I had no arms or legs and my head was shaped like a hemisphere. I couldn't move but I could somehow see where I was. I found I was nestled in the middle of a hoard of mushrooms, within a forest I'd never seen before.

The Darkening Season

Halloween Haiku

Naked through the town,
no one can see him darting.
The pink ghost moves fast.

Spider scuttling on,
his web dusted far away.
Replaced with a fake.

The backward faced freak.
Always looking out behind,
but ghouls are in front.

Glowing pumpkin face.
Too hot inside for real life,
but still they live on.

The Darkening Season

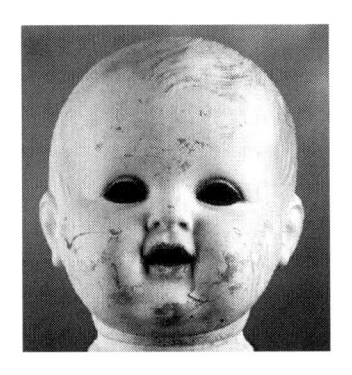

The Doll

Charles was fed up with women. Why wouldn't they have anything to do with him? Sure, he didn't like washing and never cleaned his teeth but surely, he still deserved to be loved?

Mabel lived directly opposite him and he often watched her through the window. He might have been interested in a date with her if it wasn't for the strange doll she'd had delivered. It looked exactly like a real baby and he laughed as she swished down the road with it in a fancy push chair. Once he sat next to her on the bus and just stared at the rubber infant.

'He doesn't move much,' Mabel had said, discreetly covering her nose.

Charles let one rip, just to make a point.

A year later Charles was dead and was surprised to find out he was a ghost, just floating around. He was hanging around his old street when he saw Mabel pushing the pushchair. Suddenly he had an idea, he floated into the air and forced himself into the slightly open mouth of the rubber baby. He looked through its eyes from the inside and felt like he had a body again, even though he couldn't move it.

He was surprised at how much he enjoyed being submerged in the baby bath that evening, and he loved cuddling up to Mabel in bed.

'You're a pretty baby,' said Mabel gently kissing his nose.

Charles had never been happier and decided to reside inside the doll permanently.

The Darkening Season

Martin P Fuller

Martin P. Fuller is just the right side of sixty. A law enforcement officer for nearly thirty-five years, he retired and has wandered through several other jobs which have included beer salesman and delivery driver.

He started writing nearly four years ago when he started at a creative writing class at Otley near his home in Menston, Yorkshire.

Since then he has collected writing courses and groups as others collect stamps. His preferred writing is either comedy or the darker twisted tales that cause unease before midnight.

The Darkening Season

Rural Psychopath

My victims doze in sun drenched dreams,
My scythe is swift, no tell-tale screams,
The corn stalk bereft of its golden head,
Sliced in two, I ensure it's dead.

Rye nodding peacefully in the breeze of dusk,
I cut and turn its grain to rusk,
Grinding stalks beneath my boots,
My pitchfork slashing tender roots.

I hunt the barley in stalking manner,
Reduced to pulp by a big lump hammer,
In my rural crusade, I'm a lone vigilante
Eating their ears with those beans and Chianti.

I stamp out weird patterns in the crop,
Alien voices guide me, I cannot stop,
I shred the wheat, rip out the chaff
Oats they fear my frenzied laugh.

The Darkening Season

Corn on cob, terrified maze,

Become thick porridge in psychotic phase

I'm Jack the Scarecrow, nemesis of the miller

Ready to reap, I'm a cereal killer!

Green Man

October 27th, 11:56pm

The large van sped down the quiet country lane, its lights on full beam. Manny was late and he couldn't afford the grief that a late delivery would bring. He knew about the delays the burst water main had brought on the main road that week but a road atlas had revealed this Moor Lane as a detour, a few miles longer yes, but the chances of delays were negligible. His planning had paid off. His deliveries had been on time and allowed for some early finishes.

It helped that he'd borrowed some 'ROAD CLOSED' and 'ACCESS ONLY' signs from other road works. Manny had placed them at each end of Moor lane. The trick would be discovered eventually, but till then he had the road to himself and was able to put his foot down.

The Darkening Season

Tonight however, fate had intervened. There on a sharp left hand bend was a set of traffic lights just changing to red. Barriers and cones led off around the corner. He couldn't chance it. He knew the road became a slope on the other side of the bend and the stone wall and trees obscured his view of any vehicles' headlamps. If he chanced running the light it could go horribly wrong. He had to wait.

Time ticked on. He glanced at his van's dash clock. 11.55pm. The factory was only five minutes away. The lights went green and Manny sped off, just making his delivery before midnight. His trip back was uneventful the traffic light being in his favour.

October 28th. 11.57pm

Manny fumed and swore at the red light that shone at his approach. Moor Road was deserted yet the lights stayed a solid red. He'd been waiting nearly five minutes now.

His patience left him and he'd started to set off, when headlamps ahead, flashing furiously. Swearing profusely, he backed up, allowing the large lorry to pass.

Manny breathed hard. That had been stupid and dangerous. The job was great but was it worth taking chances like that? The traffic light changed. As he passed the emerald green light he saw that some joker had drawn a face on the illuminated lens. 'Everyone thinks he's a Banksy,' thought Manny.

The Darkening Season

October 29th. 11.58pm

'Damn, change you bugger change.' The light ignored his pleas. He would be late and even worse the delay would be noted by that bloody foreman who he knew had it in for him.

The traffic light had gone to red just as he'd neared the roadworks. They must be out of sequence as a vehicle was already approaching. He'd screeched to a halt just in time. Thank God, he had. It was a cop car. Country plod doing his country beat. Time ticked on.

The light finally went to green but as he started forward he fully saw the face displayed on the lamp's surface.

It was well drawn with fine detail. It appeared to be smiling. Not like one of those gormless Emoji faces but more…more cruel. Yes, cruel and spooky. The face had a mane of leaves around its head and evil eyes that appeared to follow him as he drove past. Manny shivered and stamped on the accelerator anxious to get away.

October 30th. 11:59pm

Here he was again. The lights at red for over six minutes now. He'd already been delayed picking up the stuff at the depot and now this. Manny had had a right bollocking from the foreman last night and now he was going to get shafted again.

He'd been tempted to try another route, but the water board were still digging up the main street and it looked like a car had crashed into one of the lorries at the road works. Traffic was static. Bloody traffic jam at near midnight. He was such a bloody lucky guy. He was drawn to the face on the green lens, a dull watcher in the night. On impulse, he jumped from the cab, the engine still chugging over and went towards the traffic light.

He studied the face's features in the light from the van's headlamps. He had to admit it was a clever bit of art. It was like a tree man that he'd seen in one of those garden centres. A man's face with plants woven into the features. The evil smirk seemed bigger and a defect in the green glass gave a glint to one of the eyes. He reached out to touch the image, the icon of his delay. In an instant, the light went green and the face stared down fully illuminated and scaring the shite out of him. He felt complete and utter fear. The face appeared to stand out from the glass like one of those 3D pictures and he swore he could hear laughter in the air.

Manny ran, jumped in the cab and drove off as fast as the van could go. He grazed the side walls and the grass verge, but he didn't care. Even the argument that developed later with the foreman and the threat of dismissal couldn't wipe away the fear he'd felt on the Moor Road.

He was on his last chance but no way would he use that road again, even if this was the last day of the work contract. No way.

October 31st close to Midnight

He was on the Moor Road again. He'd set off early, but the depot order was cocked up again and the van hadn't been loaded till half eleven. Then the late-night bus in front of him had hit one of his purloined road signs that had been knocked into the road by

The Darkening Season

the Moor Road junction. Its front tyres were punctured and it had skidded across the road blocking it completely.

No matter what, he'd be late but he knew the foreman was delayed himself at some family do that he'd heard mention of from the staff in the factory's loading bay. If he was there and unloading by quarter past twelve he'd be safe.

The expectation of the red traffic light, and the prospect of beholding the eyes of the drawn man frightened him, but it was Hobson's choice. Wait till the bus was moved or Moor Road.

He drove onto Moor Road as fast as the engine and gears could manage.

As he travelled he saw the lights and as expected, they shone a ruby red, like a shiny drop of blood in the night.
Suddenly, miraculously, they changed. Red, amber and then green.

'YES!' shouted Manny as he dropped a gear and sped past the traffic light at fifty.

'At last. At last I'm past that shite'.

Just around the corner and down the hill. His luck had changed at last.

November 1st. 8am

The ambulance had removed the broken body from the scene after it had been cut from the wreckage by the firemen. The van was a heap of crushed metal, welded into the front of the heavy lorry it had collided head on with. The lorry driver had escaped injury, he was just shaken up. The van driver was a shattered corpse.

P.C Carl Robson had managed to get some of the preliminary story from the lorry driver.

The Darkening Season

'The van just belted around the corner on my side of the road. I couldn't do anything. The lorry's battery or something had packed up. I didn't have lights or hazards. Everything had just gone out. He didn't even see me till it was too late'.

Carl walked back down the route the van had taken, past the short skid marks left on the road as the van driver had finally seen the stationary lorry.

Why he'd been driving so fast and on the wrong side of the road would probably never be known.

Carl came across cones, barriers and a set of traffic lights which had been dropped by highway contractors by the road's edge before it had been closed by the police.

Maybe it had been a trick of the light, but Carl could have sworn the lights were on and the bright green light appeared to show a man's face, covered in leaves, laughing. The red light also shone with a man's face twisted in terror. Both were so beautiful yet terrifying. He looked around puzzled. There was no generator to power the lights. When he looked back at the traffic lights, they were dark with no trace of any image on their dusty lenses.

Carl turned, unsettled and walked past the ancient green woods bordering the road towards the place of sacrifice.

The Darkening Season

A Halloween for Henry

Henry lit the thirteenth black candle then, adjusting his hood to shadow his face, couldn't help but take an admiring peek at himself in the dark wood mirror on the wall. He looked so chic in the black silk gown, with its silver threaded occult symbols.

It had cost an absolute bomb of course, and he still couldn't believe the price of black candles. It was unfair when at Christmas he could get bargains on red, white and blue candles with all sorts of Christmassy things on, but mention black candles for a black mass and the prices soared. Worse still, if he mentioned he was into black magic he would be directed to the chocolate aisle.

Still it was all worth it he thought as he closed his dark velvet curtains across his bedroom window. His mum was out at bingo then staying over at his Auntie Millie's. He would have the whole house to himself for his Halloween celebration. A celebration that would lead to him to obtaining ultimate demonic

The Darkening Season

power and all the respect he was due. Girls would flock to him and men would to fear him.

The flickering candle light gave his dreams a thrilling excitement and a brilliant eerie atmosphere. He had even swapped his 'Batman the Dark Knight' electric chronometer for the hall clock that chimed in very loud clangs. When midnight arrived the tolling of its bells would be really dramatic. Brill.

It was a quarter to midnight and the anticipation was delightful.

He decided to check his equipment yet again. The Devil was in the detail. (How he loved that phrase).

He'd locked the doors and turned off all the lights. His ottoman was covered in a spare black velvet curtain and he'd made an upside down cross from two black painted twelve-inch rulers stuck in a big ball of plasticine.

On his covered ottoman was his Mothers best silver salver, minus its assorted tea pot and bowls. On its shiny bright surface, lay his ceremonial knife. Another bloody expense but luckily on sale at his local Tesco's. It had earned him double points too, although all the fuss and palaver to prove he was over twenty-one had been embarrassing. Once he had been blessed with supreme occult power he would curse the supermarket with a plague of rats or spiders, or make the cheese go out of date.

He had sharpened the knife until it would slice through any flesh it touched. That thought drew him towards Twinky the hamster hidden beneath a mound of straw in its cage. He'd read the stories of young virgins tied to satanic altars, with the spooky chanting of devil worshippers…. chanting Latin things…and other, well… sort of…. chants. But apart from himself he didn't know of any virgins so he'd thought about sacrificing a black cockerel instead. The price the local farmer wanted was a rip off,

The Darkening Season

especially when you could get a big roasting chicken and trimmings in the supermarket for less than a tenner, and again earn loyalty points. That farm too would suffer his wrath.

However, his funds being low because of the candles, curtains, gown and knife, he had lowered his sights a little.

Alan Roberts, a real wanker from college, had sold him his pet hamster for three quid and half a bottle of his mum's sherry. Alan had failed to tell him Twinky was one sick hamster. In fact, so sick it was a blessing that in…. yes, eleven minutes, it would be put out of its misery whilst at the same time, Henry would receive the power of all the Hells. Power, power, power. He couldn't say it enough times.

Now Henry got out his real prize. The grimoire. He'd found it in an old book shop down the high street that was closing down and a lot of stuff was on sale. He'd looked through a lot of books but somehow he'd been drawn to one that proclaimed it was an illustrated ladies medical dictionary. Thinking there would be pictures of women in the nuddy, he had surreptitiously flicked through the pages. He'd been ecstatic when he realised it was a real book on black magic and frightening necromantic spells. Oh joy!

It had cost him £6.66 pence, an odd amount that seemed somehow familiar. He was too relived to consider how lucky he was. Usually magic books would have cost most of his crap wage he got from the telesales job, which he detested and was also marked, along with Roddy Thomas his idiot supervisor, to be decimated by….by something that was so terrible that he could not bring himself to think of it at that moment. But would soon.

Once he'd got it home he realised the book was the answer to all his dark prayers. It was written in a strange language, possibly Latin. However, inserted into the pages were notes

The Darkening Season

written in English. Old style English in flowery handwriting that used a lot of 'thou's' and 'thee's' but with effort, understandable. It had taken three months to finish the book's translation and make his own notes but at the end he felt he could understand the rituals the book described.

It was five minutes to mid-night. Time for Twinky to realise the great honour he was to receive.

He opened the cage door ready for a sudden rodent escape. None came so he delved into the straw for the little animal. His hand touched fur and he grasped the creature, quickly drawing it out of the cage and placing it on the silver salver. Twinky fell over onto its back, its little legs pointing stiffly upwards. It was quite dead.

Henry swore and danced around the room in a rage. He vowed that Alan Roberts fate would be sealed in dark flowing blood and boils. His rage transformed to despair and he fretted about what to do. The ceremony demanded a blood sacrifice at the stroke of twelve, now only two minutes away.

Then Henry remembered Maurice, his mother's angel fish. It was the lone survivor of a shoal of fish in his late father's fish tank. It was lovingly fed by his mum, who regarded it as a second son.

He looked at Twinky, in the advanced stages of rigor-mortis. It was a no brainer.

He dashed into his mother's bedroom, and used the soft sieve to lift out a wriggling Maurice. Another sprint into his bedroom and Maurice was soon flapping about on the silver tray, just as the last seconds ticked down to midnight.

Henry began to chant the ritual, holding his transcribed notes in front of him and wishing his handwriting was better. There was certainly Latin in amongst the words but it also had

The Darkening Season

Greek and according to the old notes from the book, Babylonian. He had no idea what the words really meant, but they sounded really, really cool. He felt so grown up

The hall clock began to sound its chimes of midnight. Henry's chant was repeated in a louder voice. He was aware of the candles flickering and strange shadows fluttered across his Iron Man and Hulk posters.

'Bugger!' he exclaimed in the middle of a chanting phrase. 'I forgot to light the incense. Never mind, it probably won't matter, but ooh I said 'bugger' in the spell ritual. I hope that won't spoil the magic'.

Henry carried on chanting, a little faster now to make up for the time he had lost focus.

As the final chime of the midnight hour struck, Henry raised his knife then plunged it down towards the purloined fish. As the tip touched the first tiny scale there was a flash of bright green light, then every candle blew out.

There was a black silence.

Poor Henry. The book had chosen well in finding a willing virgin with an IQ only just into the double figures. Its pages slowly closed, trapping its parchment translations. Henry's notes glowed then burnt away to white ash, just as Henrys curtains fell from their pole to lie on a floor of thirteen cooling pools of black wax. Poor Maurice spared the knife, expired from shock and an acute lack of water.

It was dawn when the sun's first rays entered Henry's bedroom and touched upon a small furry rodent. Twinky twitched then rolled over onto its paws, its image mirrored in the silver salver. With great fastidiousness, it began to clean its fur with tiny paws. Its efforts hampered by the little dark robe with silver patterns it wore, and a little hood covering its cute ears.

The Darkening Season

As it gazed into its reflection on the silver salver, Twinky stopped its cleaning and admired itself. For a hamster, he really looked quite chic.

The Darkening Season

The Darkening Season

Gearr

I am a Druid and Gaerr is my name.
Gearr, the Hare, the Shape-shifter,
bringing the benefits of balance,
intuition and the promise of fulfilment.
I am a gatekeeper, walking between worlds,
working with Merlin to travel the land
of the ancestors and gain
knowledge and wisdom.

Those that need me find me.

www.druidry.org

The Darkening Season

The Last Harvest

Long ago in ages past, before the Romans came to our lands and brought Christianity, our ancestors celebrated Samhain, the end of summer. The last harvest before winter. It was a time when man lived in balance with his environment.

At Samhain the sheep were brought down from the hill pastures, the cattle from the lowland fells and decisions were made about life and death. It was the time of the great sorting. The sorting of which animals belonged to which family.

The men of each family had to decide which of their precious animals to slaughter for the oncoming winter's food. Hard, tough decisions had to be made.

Should it be Kyle, the old bull? Could he manage another season? Were the young bulls ready?

Should it be Rose. Who was weary now and lame, but had birthed eight good calves in as many years, but perhaps her meat would be tough.

What about Edna? The young heifer who was malnourished and thin. She was from good breeding stock but if she could survive

The Darkening Season

the winter then she had time to fill out with the new spring grass and be ready for the kill at next Samhain. Una was always wandering off taking valuable time to find her. Then there was Kenna who bullied the heifers and gave them no peace. Flora had produced many calves but was distrusted by the others and so had become excluded from the companionship of the herd. Wise old Gilic kept the herd together when the weather was bad. There was the maiden Ribhinn, no not Ribhinn, she was next year's breeding stock. Greer was alert to danger and protected them all. Blair specialised in searching out the best herbs and grasses and produced very high quality rich milk.

Perhaps Bruadran the dreamer? He spent little time eating and was thin, but a thin bullock wouldn't feed the family all winter. Then there was Drusilla who always seemed to make herself invisible at this time of sorting. Um! Perhaps no more.

It was always a mistake to give them a name.

Decisions were made and cattle slaughtered. The blood was drained off and the hides removed. The meat was chopped up, sliced and battered into the right shapes, coated and soaked in salt, before being hung over the fires to dry. The smell of the drying dead flesh would linger in their nostrils for days. The feet were removed and boiled up for glue. Buttons would be moulded from the hooves. Sinews and ligaments were stretched and dried for ropes of all kinds, the finer sinews pulled tight for sewing threads. Tongues removed, squashed into pots, prodded and poked and boiled up as a delicacy for the men of the family. Heart, liver, intestines and kidneys were doused in various herbs and laid out to dry and used by the wise women of the villages for healing of all kinds. The hide was scraped and salted and treated with all sorts of preparations and dyes before it was hung outside on racks of wood and left to dry in the last of the sunny days. But the sun could be

The Darkening Season

fickle at this time of year and had a habit of hiding behind the damp clouds as it journeyed to rise in the South East in time for the Winter Solstice. So the women had to be quick and nimble in their work. The winter solstice was only six weeks away.

Finally the work was done, after the fat had been rendered down for burning oil and candles, all that was left were the bones. The good ones were boiled, simmered down with various herbs and spices and then left to stew all winter in the large family cooking pot, where various pieces of dried meat and vegetables would be added each day. But there were always waste bones. Bones that were too old, too brittle or too diseased to be useful.

These leftover bones were loaded onto carts and ferried by the cart load to specially dug out pits at the edges of the villages. Here the bones were piled high, fat thrown on them, thanks given to the animals for the giving of their lives. Then the ancestors were honoured and asked to receive the souls of those fallen and take then back to the Summerlands.

The BONE FIRES were lit. Samhain was here, the hard work was over and now it was a time for feasting and celebrations.

BONE FIRES are now called BONFIRES !

The Darkening Season

Stepping Back

At Samhain the veil between our worlds is thin and I passed easily into the other world and journeyed to the land of my ancestors. It was 590 AD.

I could sense fear and panic in the air. I was riding a black cob at speed along dirt tracks, through villages, over bogs and grassy meadows. Danger was close and the settlements had to be warned to take to the hills with their livestock, take their valuables and run and run and run. The air was thick with confusion, people rushing and pushing and screaming in fear.

With me were my companions, all of us warriors, clothed in our wolf skins and long leather boots, our knives securely fastened to our knotted belts and shields clanking against our sword hilts. As we rode, the valley bottom gave way to spring meadows, then across the South Tyne and the steep hills which eventually took us to the cliff tops. We lined up next to each other, warrior to warrior, our horses shuffling and snorting as they took their positions.

The Darkening Season

We were all heaving with sweat, out of breath and afraid but, more than that, we were angry, very angry and as the anger grew we began shouting. Then this shouting changed to the chantings of our war song, banging on our shields in rhythm to our chant we sang ….

"We are Tweddles. Men of the Tweed. Men of the Tweed. Men of the Tweed"

And far away in the distance as the blanketing fog began to lift and gaps appeared we could see them clearly THE VIKING SHIPS.

And I knew at this point that I was home. I had been here before, at this time and in this place. I had been a Border Reiver, part of a clan of Northmen who had fought for our land.

I had returned to the land of my ancestors.

As I stood acknowledging who I was I became aware that I was slipping back through the veil to the present time.

The Darkening Season

The Menacing Spines

When laying the hedge:
Hawthorn, gnarled and tough
Birch, friendly and pliable,
Holly, prickly and fierce
Wild Rose, twists and turns,
Elder, brittle and stubborn.
But Willow goes with the flow.
And all the while
the Blackthorn
awaits her turn
to be pleached and laid.
With spines erect and sharp
she stabs and punctures
the hand, draws blood
and yet stirs not!
Respect she calls. Respect …..
The message sent
and poison flows.

The Darkening Season

Cailleach

(ky och)

As the green mantle
leaves the earth,
seeds go back
to the soil.
The hag of winter
RETURNS,
Blue black faced
with only one eye,
matted brushwood hair
and scarlet red teeth,
Bringer of death,
Rider of wolf
traversing the skies,
Commander of weather,
collector of storms,
blizzards and ice.
Clothed in snow
she blankets the hills,
cleansing the land.
She blusters with power.
Also the midwife
of the dying year,
Guardian of seed,
of what is yet
to come
held warm beneath

The Darkening Season

her feet,
Keeper of the life force
of rebirth and Beltaine,
Symbol of transformation.
BEWARE!
The Cailleach lives within us all.

The Darkening Season

The Blackthorn

Winter descends;
Samhain!
The solar year
beckons our energies inward.
We must enter our
unconcious world,
face shadows
of dark demons.
We call to the
purging Blackthorn
to open clear pathways
through our inner world,
to shift blockages,
overcome our negative fears
and push us closer
to our karmic selves.

The Darkening Season

Samhain Weather.

Mist
early morn,
softening the trees,
rising from the dew soaked fields,
first thickening then
fleeing the
sun

Sun
arises
on the autumn morn
evaporating the dew
hiding in the mist
then bursting
forth.

Crisp
fresh morning
mist in the valley
frost grips my nose and fingers
The Golden Sun rises
clear blue sky
peace

The Darkening Season

The Darkening Season

Jo Campbell

Jo is a fiction writer with a passion for all things spooky and mysterious.

Having written very little since leaving School she was inspired to take it up seriously after attending a WEA Creative writing group 3 years ago.

Jo's writing is the result of daydreams and nightmares! An Essex girl by birth she has lived in the shadow of the Yorkshire moors since the age of 13.

Besides reading and writing Jo likes sunshine, football, films and wine.

The Darkening Season

Candyland. The legend of Redboy.

Halloween at Candyland had always been spectacular. This year would be no exception. All the kiosks were stocked with sweet treats and the Park attendants were also heavily armed with the sugary stuff.

Darkness descended, pumpkins and lanterns were lit and the park rides were in full swing. The noise squealed in and around the place, swirling with the roundabouts, weaving up, down and around with the rollercoasters.

Most of the children were dressed up wearing costumes ghoulish and garish, stuffing their overfilled mouths with more free chocolate, jellies and candy sticks. Adults too, greedily pushed through crowds to fill their buckets and bellies with sweets and candy they could probably do without.

The music of the Theme park villains began to drift through the night air signalling the start of the eagerly anticipated parade. Adults gripped the hands of their children tightly as they swarmed towards the roped off areas.

The Darkening Season

From all corners a swathe of new Park attendants appeared, gliding through the throng with tempting trays of candy.
"Candy for the children, candy for the children!" They called.

Some of the children were still in the shops and around the stalls, shouting "Trick or treat?" holding out their buckets for more sweets and ignored the calls from outside.

An angry crackle of static jolted through the radios of the attendants who were instructed to quickly guide the children away from the shops and back into the crowd. Robotically, they turned, in unison, to face the outer edges of the park and headed towards the shops the smell of sweet sticky candy billowing from their trays.

"C'mon kids you'll miss the parade. Come out and get a good view. We've tons of magic villain candy here."

The children stopped, turned and followed their noses straight for the trays of tempting sweetness.

Frantically the attendants distributed candy, seeking out each and every child presenting the beautiful dark chocolate shells filled with dripping red jelly.

The music from the parade became louder as it, progressed through the park.

The attendants rose up and called, "Do you wanna see Redboy? Yell if you wanna see Redboy?"

The swelling crowd surged towards the attendants, children craving more candy and chanting for Redboy, as they were whipped up into a frenzy and encouraged to "Eat his candy, call his name."

The scary theme park characters danced their way into the central arena. The colours of the costumes and songs of the 'villains' were heady and intoxicating, the grip of hands between adult and child loosened as they were all encouraged to clap, wave, hiss and boo; and, of course, chant for Redboy, the biggest villain of all.

There he was, towering at the top of the highest carriage, the one the children wanted to see; Redboy, the shiny scarred cracked and eyeless demon child. The legend of Candyland.

He opened his arms to the staring crowd and bowed his head, uttering the single word, "Children."

With that puffs of red smoke rose in thick clouds from under the park attendants' cloaks holding the crowds in awe.

Sweet notes from a flute began to play and a marching drum signalled the parade was coming to its climax.

Then the drums stopped, the flute's melodies faded and the smoke cleared. The adults looked around for their children.

They were gone. All that was left was a sticky redness oozing on the ground, and the faintest sound of a flute in a far-off place.

Oh, and of course, the legend of Red boy

The Darkening Season

The Corridor.

It was October 31st. Dolly had, what she hoped, was her last Hospital visit today.

It was just a short distance from home to hospital for her and she never paid much attention to how she got there, her mind was always on when she could leave. She started each journey with anticipation and ended it with deep disappointment knowing she had to go back again.

This time was different though. She was certain she would finally be discharged today.

Dolly entered through the heavy swing doors. The corridor always seemed longer than it looked. She smelled the intoxicating liquor of antiseptic mixing with the sounds of crisp rustling starched uniforms and the heavy rolling wheels of the trolleys. No one really spoke to each other along this corridor but Dolly didn't mind. She was tired of seeing the place.

The end of Autumn had brought a raw dampness and Dolly felt cold, colder than she had felt in a long time. Shivering, she paused to wrap her coat around herself. The surrounding air felt

The Darkening Season

thin and the outside gloom of fog seemed to descend inside the corridor.

As Dolly approached the waiting room she heard her name called. Looking up she saw the smiling face of the 'special' Nurse. Everyone wanted to be assigned this Nurse, that was a clear indication that this was the final visit. No more pacing the corridor, no more disappointment in the waiting room.

"Ah Dolly. This way darlin'." The nurse said. Dolly took her hand suddenly feeling weightless and free as she transcended the thin veil of mist.

The Darkening Season

The Winter Babies.

Gnarly branches of the oak tree troubled by the weight of Autumn's end creaked and bent towards the ground.

Grey dusk had descended and the huddled figure wrapped a grubby shawl tightly around her body and the bundle she carried.

Kneeling at the trunk of the tree she bowed her head briefly muttering a few words. She turned her head and checked she had not been followed then unwrapped her bundle rolling the contents onto the ground.

She took a small shovel and began to dig, carefully removing an area of grass to use as a cover later. Task complete she brushed herself down and scurried away.

On her way home, she passed through the slum quarters of the Capital, quickening her step, wary of the late hour. Even so, she was startled when she felt a hand on her shoulder.

"It's me. Was it? Did it work out?"

"Oh, Martha love, you give me a fright! Yes darlin' all is well. You'll be owing me the rest now."

The Darkening Season

The woman licked her lips as Martha dropped coins into her dirty hands. Their eyes met, Martha's questioning.

"I fell down, can't see so well in the dark. Best be gettin' on home girl. It's a cold 'un tonight."

It was indeed a cold night. The woman shivered by her fire and gave the coal a poke. She pulled her chair nearer the flames and poured another large glass of port, raising it in toast.

"The Winter Babies."

She snorted the drink down, warm and drunk she slept, only to be woken by tapping and clawing sounds on her windows. Stumbling over she rubbed the icy panes with her sleeve. Hard rain, like bare branches scraped and scratched, the moon dipped in and out of the clouds like a tiny white face.

The screams and howls of the wind and rain became louder, she drank more port to drown out the sounds and passed out, face down onto the bed, where she awoke the next morning to the baying of an angry mob outside in the street. Intrigued she went to see what the commotion was and was horrified to see her home surrounded.

A smash told her they were trying to get in. She ran to bolt her door but was stopped by what she saw through the window.

She could see where the storm had hit the higher ground. The relentless, lashing rain had washed away land at the roots of the tree on the hill. Exposing her, exposing them.

Carried in the arms of the grieving townsfolk her secret was laid bare. A procession of those sold to her. Poor infants whose desperate mothers thought they were going to a better life with childless rich folk.

The storm had delivered the Winter Babies.

The Darkening Season

Laura Driver

I got into writing through blogging and I got into blogging through a need to write about my family life and record the lives of my two children, a step daughter, two dogs and a husband.

My blog **www.arewenearlythereyetmummy.com** will be a legacy for them. I then set up a more personal and poignant blog, A mum shaped hole, in which I explore the effect on my life of losing my mother when I was nine years old.

I joined the creative writing group in Otley to expand my writing skills and through the influence and encouragement of James Nash and the group I have stepped out of my comfort zone and have enjoyed writing fiction of various genres.

The Darkening Season

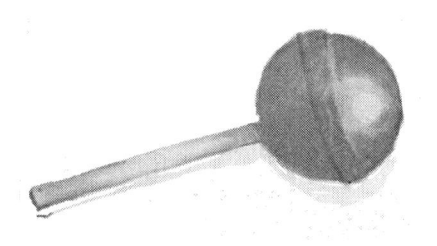

Autumn 1987

My friend Catherine blows out eight candles before we gather on the carpet, a sea of pretty party dresses fill the room. We play a final party game of 'who can suck the fruit pastille the longest'.

The phone rings. Catherine's Mum leaves the room. Moments later she returns and for a second we lock eyes. I stop sucking my sweet and chew it, promptly failing the game.

A flurry of parents arrive signalling the end of the celebration. My Dad, who is always on time arrives last. Maria gives my Dad an uncharacteristic hug on the doorstep, and says she's sorry.

Sorry for what?

As we begin the short walk home I unwrap a sticky yellow lollipop from my party bag. I talk about the party; the cake, the games, the presents but I want to talk about something else. I ask how Mum is.

He ignores me or doesn't hear my question. "How is Mummy?"

I ask again.

The Darkening Season

Nothing. He is looking straight ahead and our pace quickens. Why won't he speak to me? My stomach churns and I ask him louder.

He stops and bends down so that his eyes are level with mine. There is sadness in his eyes. Something is wrong, my Daddy looks different. He is holding my hand tight. I think I already know. The lollipop falls from my hand, my knees start to give way.

"Laura, mummy has died."

I want to be sick. Hot tears roll down my cheeks and the pavement falls away from my feet as my Dad scoops me up. I look at the lollipop lying on the ground; its sticky coating covered in grit.

I am nine years old. My Mummy has gone.

The Darkening Season

Six

Six. The number of low Autumn moons Carol Montgomery had seen through the triple-glazed velux window in the attic and the way she measured the length of her captivity.

Two moons ago she'd made herself hoarse from shouting for help. Who would hear her anyway? Her ex-husband had soundproofed the attic when, in the early throes of a mid-life crisis, he'd bought a set of drums. A motorbike, a woman half his age and the end of their marriage had followed.

Frightened and alone she worried how her kids were coping without her. Hot tears rolled down her face. She blew her snotty nose on her pyjama sleeve. She didn't know when it would end, or how. Her captors were volatile, at best.

Once a day they slid a tray into the room with a Pot Noodle (chicken and mushroom) and a couple of slices of Marmite on toast. She hated Marmite. Each time the tray arrived she'd begged for her release, she'd promised the earth, but all she got was steely silence.

On the morning after the ninth moon she awoke to find the door ajar. Was it over or were they playing with her? Bracing herself she went down the stairs. The house was a mess. Clothes,

The Darkening Season

dishes and general detritus littered each room she passed and every bloody light in the house was on.

She found them sat at the kitchen table glued to their mobile phone screens. Jack, the oldest of her teenage twins by twenty three minutes, looked up from his phone and with a look of contempt spoke.

"I hope you've learnt your lesson. Maybe you'll think twice before shutting off the wifi again".

The Darkening Season

Deathly Delights

The body lay prone, on the pavement. Congealed blood pooled among unnaturally splayed limbs. The beads of the victim's necklace had scattered like marbles and were being bagged by a forensic pathologist. The witnesses, who had been in a board meeting in the neighbouring office block, had all corroborated that the woman had appeared on the roof of the building where she stood momentarily, before simply stepping off.

When police officers had knocked on his door and asked him to sit down, so that they could tell him the bad news, Mark was obviously distressed. Newly married with their future ahead of them he had explained, to the sympathetic faces, that Judy had never given any indication that she was depressed or had any suicidal tendencies. It was her birthday and that morning she'd been her usual chirpy self. She'd given him a kiss and set off for work wearing the gift he'd just given her, a stunning necklace.

As the officers left he agreed, through a veil of tears, to identify Judy's body formally the following day. Mark dried his eyes on his sleeve as he sat in the kitchen making a list of people

The Darkening Season

he needed to call. But first things first – he lifted his laptop screen and headed onto the Dark Web to leave a thoroughly deserved five star review for 'Deathly Delights' the website where he bought the necklace. The description had simply said, "In an unhappy relationship? Gift this necklace to your partner and all your problems will fall away."

The Darkening Season

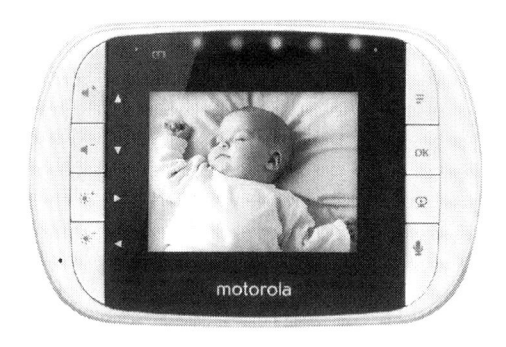

Overheard

"Mummy, mummy, is that you?" Sarah awoke bolt upright, heart pounding, blinking into the darkness. Aware of a crackling noise on the baby monitor, she gave it a whack.

The jagged edges of her nightmare slowly prodded her, a reminder of the torment. A faceless creature had taken her son and she could only watch, paralysed as they got further away. Her skin prickled.

The nightmare ebbed giving way to relief. The baby monitor continued to crackle. It was the only way she could hear Sammy, at night, on the floor above. He hadn't called out for her in months, but she needed to know that if he did she would hear.

She struck the monitor again, this time the crackling stopped. Sarah lay back down, it was 3.10 am. She could get a few more hours before Sammy would pounce on her, begging to watch CBeebies.

Sleep was washing over her when a shrill scream propelled her out of bed. Without thinking Sarah was flying up the stairs, two at a time.

The Darkening Season

She opened Sammy's door and flicked the light on, casting a strip of pale yellow over the empty bed where his crumpled duvet lay.

Trembling Sarah looked down at the monitor which was clasped tightly against her chest. It crackled and then a voice, Sammy's voice "Who are you? Where's my mummy?"

The Darkening Season

The Darkening Season

Polly Smith

Two years ago I decided to explore the world of creative writing with the 'Otley Writers'. The humour, talent and support from the Group has inspired me to keep going.

To date writing has become a favourite pastime that triggers interest in all manner of topics.

I also enjoy walking, playing golf, learning to play bridge and spending time with family and friends.

The Darkening Season

Season's Chill

"Another pint bro?" Jim asked as the weather warning flashed up on the TV screen. He glanced out of the pub window. The landscape was carpeted in thick layers of white velvet. Trees majestic in stance, their branches half sleeved in snow towered protectively over the picturesque landscape. But the beauty of snow concealed a terrifying reality. This was a village frozen in the cruel grip of nature's icy chill. A village weighed down by a shroud of hysterical misery.

There'd been a week of snow followed by freezing temperatures. Police and volunteers were frantically searching for three missing children. Their disappearance was a mystery. After three days, hope of finding them alive was fading.

Jim looked back at the weather report. 'Further snow expected before a slow thaw at the weekend'. His pub was a welcome refuge for the volunteers. A place where they could congregate and offer support to one another and keep up with police and press releases. Jim made sure there was a roaring fire and plenty of hot food available.

Keith knocked back the last dregs of his pint. "No, I won't have another Jim, best get back out there."

The Darkening Season

Keith knew the area inside out. He'd lived and worked on the land for as long as he could remember. His local knowledge was invaluable to the search.

Like most people in the village, he knew the children well. It was unbearable seeing their happy innocent faces smiling out from the publicity posters. But it was the description of their clothing that really hit home. It seemed to emphasise their innocent vulnerability. Katy's red woolly hat with it's oversized pom-pom, Bethany's multi coloured scarf and Nathan's, 'Harry Potter' style spectacles.

Eight hours later a Boeing 737 left the ground. From the window seat Jim looked down at the frozen landscape. He knew once the thaw set in, the search would end. He closed his eyes, trying to blot out the horrifying image. Three snowmen standing in line. Their proximity to one another offered him a misplaced sense of comfort. But it was the woolly hat set at a jaunty angle, the carefully tied scarf and the black rimmed glasses that floored him.

They captured the children's tender personalities to perfection. He should know he'd taken great care to place the right item on the right child.

His thoughts turned to the pub. Perhaps his brother Keith would run it in his absence.

The Darkening Season

Memories of Autumn

Earth rotating on its axis orbiting the Sun
Defining our four seasons since time began
Golden hues of Autumn adorn the countryside
Vibrant shades of yellow, orange, green and brown.

Children wearing wellies, kicking autumn leaves
Chasing one another climbing rocks and trees
Fighting over conkers playing hide and seek
Eating juicy blackberries collected for their tea.

Darkness falls too quickly, families head back home
Dirty, happy faces - how the kids have grown
Mothers cuddle toddlers in the fading light
Fathers rescue teenagers, lost and out of sight.

The table's set for dinner, a roast for all to share
Conversation ceases as we all fill up on fare
Blackberry and apple crumble with custard – what a treat!
Homework is abandoned as conkers fight defeat.

The Darkening Season

Trick or Treat

Tick, tock, tick, tock. Time dominates my world. Nervously I fiddle with the buttons of my cardigan, my eyes willing the hands of the clock to move faster. I watch moonlit shadows dancing on the sitting room walls and sink further back into my armchair. No one would guess I was at home.

My thoughts dwell on the past as I wait for my neighbour to call. How my life has changed. I was settled here, comfortable in retirement with my dear husband Jack. Weekends spent together with our family, especially the grandchildren. How I miss the joy and laughter that filled our home. Everything was suddenly taken away. Now I live in the deafening silence of grief struggling to cope with the loneliness of their tragic loss. Summer months dragging by into the gloom of dark chilly nights.

I don't like Halloween, it frightens me. I've lost my confidence since Jack died. Nowadays I keep myself to myself and rarely venture out. The local kids think I'm a witch and taunt me with their name calling. I'm so grateful for the kindness of my neighbour. She knows I'll be nervous tonight and has kindly offered to sit with me. Even so, the doorbell startles me when it

The Darkening Season

rings. Heart pounding, I cautiously open the door and gasp in surprise. Three small children, dressed in flimsy Halloween outfits, giggle as they shiver in the darkness. I look down at their mischievous faces. "Trick or Treat?" they chant in unison. Three pairs of eyes stare up at me. Their gaze transforms into an aura of shimmering light. It slowly floats upwards blurring my vision, invading my mind as it swirls around my head. I lose any sense of control and drift into a comforting sense of warm nothingness.

Suddenly a voice calls out. "Can someone help here? Are you alright love? What happened to you? Are you lost? Don't worry I'll take care of you."

I don't understand. Are they talking to me? I'm not scared. I'm not lost, but they insist on fussing over me.

I shiver and someone drapes a coat around my shoulders before I'm led away. And now I'm bombarded with questions that befuddle me. What's my name? Where do I live? Where have I been? Over and over the questions persist. I'm surrounded by uniforms, faces, sterile places.

"Please leave me alone," I plead. I shake my head in puzzlement, then give a sigh of relief as I see a familiar face.

My daughter Jean smiles as she wraps her arms around me. She looks tired, pale and tearful and informs me I've been missing for the best part of a year. She takes me home and stays with me whilst I try to remember. Despite her concern I feel content and at peace with the world. Most nights I dream about devils, ghosts, and zombies. My dreams don't make any sense until one evening the doorbell rings and Jean answers the door. I hear children's voices chanting "Trick or Treat?" It triggers memories.

And so I sit and wait. Jean's been missing for nine months now, but no one believes my story. I can't wait for Halloween this year, when Jean returns with news of Jack and the family.

The Darkening Season

Saille

I am Druid, I am Saille pronounced 'Sayl-Yeh,' The Willow (Salix,) the tree of enchantment. I was born in April, the Celtic month of Willow. Moons ago Saille beckoned and I turned to her, and beneath the gentle fronds of her branches she whispered to me, inviting me to share her Willow ways. She bestowed gifts of perception, inspiration, creativity and flexibility, the power to bend around obstacles without discord. She taught me to use my psychic energy and the pure magic that is around me skilfully, and to understand the oracle of dreams. She showed me spiritual growth and the healing benefits of drawing my energy as she does from Mother Earth, the Sun, the flowing waters and her close association with the Moon.

I am Saille, friend of the Fae, the intuitive Seer, peacemaker and bringer of harmony.

Deep peace and the blessing of light to you.

The Darkening Season

Druid

Lifeless twigs trampled as fractured bones, she treads
Midnight Moon, forest torch, wary eyes clandestine watch
Cernunnos from dark shadows warns, *'Callers here are few,'*
Take sanctuary nocturnal friends in Hollow, Oak and Yew
Do not fear a Druid near, peaceful is her mission,
Samhain Eve, come, dead souls, a word, a touch, a vision
Ancestors ever nearer now, the ethereal veil is thin
Pitch of night, woodland world, her secret Grove within
Sacred Circle, long weather worn, a lone survivor stands
Dear aged rugged Heel Stone, souvenir of ancient lands
Druid beckons *'Spirits Step close'* from shadow into glade
Across the threshold speak to me, from beyond the grave
Tell of your Celtic wisdom, Bards, Sorcerers and Seers,
Nature's Priests, historic peers, essence with sentient ease
Oh that I could reach the wise, hear whispers on the breeze
Arms outstretched held moonward lone Druid amid the trees

The Darkening Season

Divine Hag of Winter

As a Druid Nature forms an important focus for all that we hold dear. In Nature we see the cycle of birth, life, death and rebirth. Many Druids see the changing seasons represented by a Deity, often female, a Goddess, who is all things. Born in the Spring she is the Maiden, budding, youthful, fertile, she blossoms to Mother and the Summer blooming and abundant. The wheel turns once more to the Autumn and the wisdom that comes with advancing years. Then as the leaves fall and the sun weakens, she is the Crone, the Wise Woman, The Cailleach, she who stands between the worlds.

*

The Solstice wheel turns, as it always turns and the autumn leaves begin to fall, a symbol of a life well lived before we are led to cold rest under the watchful eye of the Dark Mother, the Divine Hag of Winter.

The Darkening Season

It is Samhain, and her time. She descends across hill and valley, town and village. She is the veiled one. Her misty shroud chilling the land, skeletal trees her bones, skin, hard as frozen earth, icy streams the blood in her veins. The Hag is with us, she who stands at the gateway between the worlds. No living thing will escape her grip. Heed her wisdom! She is the Crone, the Cailleach, the repose of death, and the promise of rebirth. She is the Mother of transition who guides us from light to darkness and darkness to light.

She works her magic well, slowing the pulse of nature. Creatures rest in hollow and den as the land freezes harder, drained of all colour, scarcely breathing. Yet the Dark Mother isn't done until the land is still, silenced, shrouded in white, not a breath.

Then, just as the Moon wanes to darkness, and waxes to full light so the Divine Hag will fulfil her promise. She is midwife to the Maiden. Soon to be reborn, bursting from every hill and vale breathing life into the land. The creatures stir and the fields and forests awaken, every bud a sign of the life to come. Streams quicken as the sun gains strength, warming the earth, bringing colour and vigour to the land.

The Hag, knowing her work is done, sinks into the darkness of the Earth, where, out of sight she prepares for her return. The Solstice wheel turns as it always has until once more we feel her icy touch.

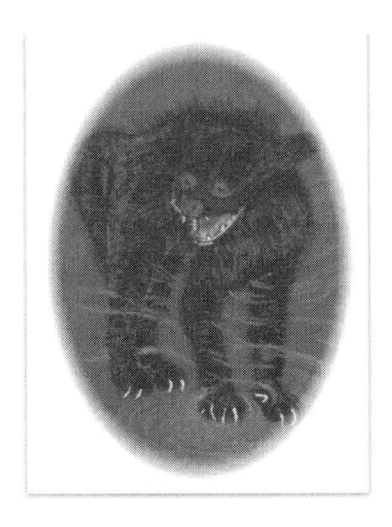

Wolfsbane

The scented tranquil water brought a rare moment of peace to Violet. She gazed entranced through the opaque glassed window at the trees swaying, shadowy, under the Samhain Moon.

Candle flames danced on the draughty sill, animating the face in the antique frame. Would he come to her tonight?

Torment returned to plague her, the Black dog of depression growling menacingly once more as she tried to make sense of the inexplicable. The mysterious illness and sudden death of her beloved John, followed closely to his grave by Aunt Agnes and then Helena.

For a brief moment her imagination dredged up healthier memories of herself and John.

The Darkening Season

Halcyon days sipping wine together in the pretty cottage garden, overflowing with blooms, herbs, vegetables and fruit trees all ripening in the summer sun. The warmth of lamp-lit winter evenings in front of the roaring fire, safe in the comfort of Johns arms. Aunt Agnes, as upright and decorous as her Queen Anne chair and the cat curled snugly on her lap, purring loudly above the comforting click of skilful needles keeping time with the tick-tock of the grandfather clock. Dear kind Aunt Agnes.

To my beloved youngest niece Violet-Jane, after all expenses and bequests have been settled, I leave the rest of my estate to her in its entirety. It is my dearest wish that 'Copse Cottage' continues to provide sanctuary for her and respite from the suffering and sorrow that has besieged her so unjustly.'

To my eldest niece Helena I leave the sum of twenty thousand pounds. Her indifference to me and hostility towards Violet has been a great sadness. For that, I insist that she must donate half of the money to a deserving charity, certainly not the church roof fund! It is my hope that my legacy teaches her the beauty of benevolence. Maybe adding a little more Jerusalem to the Jam would make for less bitterness.'

Infuriated by Aunt Agnes's acerbic wishes, Helena refused the money. Resentment was all her younger sister deserved.
Mother and Father had doted on Helena until Violet came along, stealing the love that had been exclusively hers for more than a decade. No, there would be no forgiveness.

Violet hated jam and the 'good book' had muddled her onto a very different path.

The Darkening Season

Helena hid her bitter resentment of Violet's 'Pagan ways,' behind a static mask of chaste piety. Her eyes unblinking in condemnation beneath severe scraped back hair and the cold restraint of thinly pursed lips. Violet wondered, *'Had she ever seen her sister smile'?*

Helena's death following so closely in the wake of John's and then Aunt Agnes had sent shockwaves through the village, triggering an avalanche of fumbled sympathies. Yet, this time, condolences fell on nothing more than a stony ground of relief for Violet. The facade of sisterly affection was over at last.

Helena had known for some time but didn't tell until her illness became obvious. She must have had her reasons. Certainly not to protect those around her, for she was rarely given to acts of kindness. Though she did make preserves for the church bazaar and would occasionally turn up at the cottage with jars of homemade jam, blackberry for John and plum for Aunt Agnes, in homage of her intolerance of seeds.

There was just one the one time; Violet struggled to close her mind to the agony of the memory that had returned to haunt her.

John had been overjoyed, fussing over his wife from the start.

Violet recalled the wonderful mixture of apprehension and excitement as they awaited the new arrival.

Aunt Agnes had joked that, *'It was about time the spare room was put to good use,'* and had insisted on paying for everything until the dusty old place was transformed into a charming nursery.

The Darkening Season

Nurse Abbott had brought Violet safely into the world, and generations of babies since, so it was decided that she would be in attendance.

It was an idyllic midsummer afternoon when the call came that she was required at *Copse Cottage.*

Shafts of sunlight beamed through the mullion windows as the old nurse bustled around with an air of bossy competence. Her gentle Irish brogue, playfully chastising John he should *'go downstairs and keep Aunt Agnes company before he wore the carpet out with his pacing.'* His sharp return with cups of tea and the persuasion, that *'Helena had arrived,'* was met with the nurse's matronly insistence that he keep from under her feet.

The scents of Honeysuckle, Buddleia and Lilac drifting in on the night air enhanced the mood of joyous expectation, with no hint of the horror that was about to unfold.

The gruesome memory trounced Violet's mind, cold recollection coursing through her veins. It all happened so quickly.

Dear Nurse Abbott becoming so suddenly ill, waves of nausea prompting her to take air at the window. John steadying her to the bathroom where relentless, violent, sickness rendered the old nurse incapable.

Helena had stepped in, delivering the lifeless child, whisking him away. She said she tried everything, Violet was sure she heard him cry, but Helena said not.

Violet took solace that at least now father and son were together in the afterlife. Tears trickled into the bathwater. She wondered wistfully *'How many endless tears it would take to fill*

The Darkening Season

the bath tub, until she might drown in her own grief and join them.'

The water was getting cold. She stepped out, the warm towel providing small comfort to a delicate body so fatigued by relentless sorrow.

Violet tamed her wilful red tresses into a clasp before picking up Aunt Agnes's old velvet robe from the wicker chair, fondly running her fingers over the skilfully embroidered symbols that only a Witch would understand. The robe offered a comforting closeness to Aunt Agnes and welcome warmth for her forty year old bones were no match for the rasping cold that penetrated the old cottage.

Smouldering incense hung heavy in the sitting room, mingling with squalls of bitter musty air as the old door lost its battle with the autumn chill.

Violet threw a log in the grate, captivated as a firework of hot ash burst heavenward, whilst spiteful embers escaped furtively onto the old rug.

She positioned the photograph of John on a brass pentacle in the centre of the carefully laid out altar cloth, then poured mead into a goblet and set it down. She placed candles, one black, one white, into the candelabra, fingering the solid streams of old wax that clung to the stems like frozen rivers of tears.

John smiled at her from the confines of the wooden frame. Violet closed her eyes, willing him to come to her on this night, Samhain. The night when the veil between the worlds is transparent, a perfect night to make contact with the dead.

Violet knew, as all Witches know, that such things should only be done from within the safety of a spell cast circle, with the

The Darkening Season

Goddess, God and elements of earth, air, fire and water called upon for protection.

Tonight was no exception.

Aunt Agnes had been a proficient teacher, Violet was skilful and performed her magic well, insisting that only positive energies be permitted to make contact or enter the circle.

She closed her eyes, this time in meditation, beseeching that the veil be lifted.

The cat shrieking her plea to be let out pierced the silence, jolting Violet from her spellbound contemplation. On an icy blast Luna made her escape, swiftly disappearing into the darkness.

The trees loomed like ominous shadows, stagnant in the murky gloom of an October fog that had crept in silently to shroud the night sky. Violet shuddered, pulling her robe tightly around her.

Turning the key in the rusty mortice, she pulled the heavy door curtain into place musing on Luna's frantic exit. Aunt Agnes had reared the abandoned waif to share her own dignified demeanour.

Responding to the cat's mysterious frenzy, Violet realised uneasily that she had broken the Circle, a risk she would never usually take. Without the shield of the magically protected space she was at risk from the uninvited.

Now a stale dank air had pervaded the room bringing with it a claustrophobic atmosphere.

Sensing she was no longer alone panic gripped Violet, speeding her pulse. Fearful of looking round, yet adrenalin daring her to steal a glance, she turned towards the darkened recess at the back of the room, catching sight of an intangible form lurking in the shadows. Violets mind swung between disbelief and reality. Fear crawling like ants through her veins as the apparition moved slowly ever closer.

Bringing with it the menacing stench of hatred, the shrouded figure shuffled into view.

'Helena!'

Violet recoiled in terror as the spectre of her dead sister moved closer still. Her lips thin black lines on grey marble, her accusing cavernous eyes fixed on Violet, paralysing her with fear.

Suddenly and inexplicably a book toppled from the shelf, thudding loudly at Violet's feet, swiftly followed by a splintering crash. Violet snatched the photo of John in its shattered frame from the ground clutching it to her chest, blood flowing as the pitiless shards, sliced her fingers. The pages of the book turned unaided one by one, before stopping deliberately. Violet lifted the book, smearing it with blood. *'Aconite, Wolfsbane, deadly, untraceable.'* Thoughts trounced her mind in disorientated order, before grasping the full horror of the unearthly revelation.

'Jam, Jerusalem.'

Horror and disbelief overwhelming her, Violet dared her eyes back to her ghoulish visitor.

'Poison. It was in the Jam. You poisoned John!'

Helena sneered. Her face contorted mocking.

'You killed him. You murdered my husband!'

Helena held out her arms revealing a lifeless bundle.

Violet crumpled to her knees, her pain laden cry coming from deep within the soul of a childless mother echoed in the silence.

'My baby. You killed my child!' first our son and then John'

Violet, stumbled despairingly to her feet.

The Darkening Season

'Why? Why? What could I possibly have done to you to make you destroy everything I ever loved?

Violet stared in revulsion as Helena, basking in twisted victory, smiled, her distorted. Revenge complete.

There would be no sanctuary, nor respite, no escape, her younger sister would now endure the pain of loss and loneliness, just as she had.

The next morning the late Autumn sun streamed in through the fanlight disturbing Violet into consciousness. Rising shakily, still clutching the broken frame she made her way to the bathroom.
Filling the tub she stepped in, taking the largest shard from the frame she sank deeper, drifting ever closer to John's open arms and lifeless to the crashing sounds of Helena's poltergeist fury that would forever haunt *'Copse Cottage.'*

The Darkening Season

Shape Shifter

I had my doubts about him, deceit is wrong, very wrong, dangerous in fact. I never felt we met by chance. *'Rich pickings,'* or so he thought. There's no such thing as secrets in a small town like ours. *'She's a Druid,'* didn't mean much to him then. Now though, I wonder?

I love my daily woodland walks, time to reflect, such perfect beauty, especially now, at Samhain. The fallen leaves have formed a covering of gold, orange and brown, reminding me of Grandma's carpet, the one she had on the stairs.

I thought I might modernise things after she died. In the end I didn't clear much at all from the old place, I love it just as it is.

I want to say I miss her, but you can't miss someone who's still with you. Gran was very wise, drawing knowledge from her deep love of nature, observant, quiet, a dignified woman, a Druid.

I'll not want for material things. She left everything to me, but her wise teachings mean the most.

The Darkening Season

They say the gift of magic often skips a generation. It certainly did with us. Mum left forty years ago, I've only seen her a handful of times since.

'Turns up when she wants something,' Gran would say.

I remember I resemble her, tall, brunette. I get a birthday card most years, though last year she got the date wrong. She signs, *'Vivienne (Mum)'.* The arrangement suits me fine. I'm glad it was Gran who brought me up.

I like to flow as nature flows. It feels right to be at one with all things natural and supernatural. Gran always said, *'Not all things are imagined, trust and you'll see.'* She was right of course.

I need solitude. I'm very blessed that *Broom Cottage* is on the outskirts of town and surrounded by trees. There's a stream running through the bottom of the garden. I found my Hag Stone there. I had a very contented life, everything was just right, until he brought chaos.

Gran will come to me when she needs to, her messages are always very clear. This time I'm sure I caught a glimpse of her, just for a second, she was standing near the dresser.

'Lily of the Valley' was her favourite. I love how the fragrance appears and hangs in the air, reminding me she's still near.

It was when I saw the Tarot card that I knew for sure. The rest of the deck were as I'd left them, wrapped in a purple velvet cloth in the dresser drawer. Yet there it was, 'The Seven of Swords,' the card of deception and betrayal, placed very deliberately upright in front of the photo frame.

I felt sure she meant *'him,'* that she shared my doubt and that he'd prove us right.

The Darkening Season

The time came of course he was just a little too curious. *'What plans did I have for Halloween?'* I told him, *'I'm Druid so I'll be at our Grove, and actually we don't say "Halloween" we say "Samhain."* Still he kept checking, *'Was I still going?'* Making certain I would be out.

I felt sure that he was up to something. Why did he want me out of the way? Certainly not some sweeping romantic gesture, so what? Surely he wasn't planning to rob me, take, money, jewellery? How would he get in? Break windows? No one would hear.

Our Grove is three miles away. A beautiful woodland glade on land owned by one of our group. So we're never disturbed.

Driving off I wondered, *'Did he watch me leave?* Foolish man, then he had no way of knowing that distance would mean nothing, that I work unearthly magic, that I can Shape Shift and that I would be there, high in the branches of the Oak, keeping watch with preying eyes.

I parked the car at the edge of the woods, I was wearing my white robe, I took my cloak and staff from the boot of the car and moved deftly amongst the trees. A thousand nocturnal eyes, alerted by the echo in the darkness of twigs snapping beneath my feet, watched clandestine, as I made my way deeper into the forest.

The moonlight cast shimmering shadows on the bark of the Silver Birch. The dead of night held no fear for me. I chose a tree and sat beneath her, leaning against her sturdy trunk, feeling Earth energy course through her body and mine.

I closed my eyes summoning my spirit guides, breathing deeply, feeling safe in their presence, I drifted into deep meditation. I visualised, Tawny Owl, beckoned her to come to me, to share her ways with me, so that I may become one of her kind.

A sudden shift from the stillness of meditation startled me. Cold air whirled around, I was swaying, high in the Birch tree, talons gripping the branch with great dexterity, my night vision sharp. I could see woodland creatures scurrying on the ground below. If hunger had been my mission I would have been quite the assassin.

Instead I took flight, my wings silent in the night sky, lifting me higher. The late autumn chill barely penetrating my dense plumage.

The disappearing ground became increasingly unfamiliar, yet I instinctively knew my way. Three miles is no challenge for a Tawny.

In no time I had landed on the branches of the towering old Oak, I was too high, too far away. I swooped skilfully to the Cherry Tree where I had a better view of the Cottage.

There was no one. Maybe I was mistaken. The Tarot card, the Seven of Swords, Gran was hardly ever wrong. He'll be here, so I waited as an Owl would wait, patiently for her prey.

Distracted by the wildlife below, my plumage raised like hackles, instinctively I flexed my talons, the temptation to strike diverted only by the familiar sound of the gate creaking open.

I watched him stride down the path towards the Cottage. My furious screeching pierced the night air. This was my terrain. He turned but couldn't see me, not even in the moonlight, my feathers the perfect disguise amid the trees.

It was said that Tawny Owls were the harbinger of negative magic and danger. I don't consider protecting my

The Darkening Season

territory negative magic, dangerous maybe, for him, as he was about to find out.

I screeched again and again in fury as he let himself into my Cottage. Watching as he walked from room to room, going through drawers and cupboards, opening letters, bank statements, bank books, making sure to put everything back exactly. Then the jewellery box. He took something from his pocket, an eyeglass like the one that jeweller's use. He scrutinised every last piece, yet took nothing.

One by one the lights went out, he was leaving empty handed, he had just wanted to know my finances, whether I was worth pursuing.

I waited, but he didn't appear. The bedroom lit up once more. He lifted the lid of the jewellery box, temptation had got the better of him.

Locking the door, he stepped back gazing up at the Cottage, ensuring there would be no trace of his visit.

Driven by rage, I spread my wings and took flight. I flew at him, my talons ripping into his skin, wings beating hard. I attacked again and again, tearing at him as he ran to his car. I followed for a while in silent flight before returning to the cottage.

My sharp eyes caught sight of something glinting in the moonlight at the side of the path. I swooped, picking it up and carrying it in my beak. Then began my three mile flight back to the woods.

I landed on the lower branches of the same Beech and rested. I called to my guides to channel me back and thanked the Owl for sharing her ways with me, enabling me to become one of her kind for a short time.

The Darkening Season

Then once more I was sitting in silent darkness beneath the Birch, my lips pursed tight, gripping something, Gran's ring, the antique one with the three large diamonds. I slip it on.

I need to dash, the group will be waiting.

The Samhain ritual was comforting, the veil thin and the spirit world tangibly close. I spoke to Gran, thanked her for watching over me. Afterwards we all sat around the bonfire, ate, drank and made merry, drumming, telling tales and reciting poetry.

I slept late today, missed his call. The answer phone simply said *'Sorry sweetie, will have to cancel lunch, you won't believe what's happened. Call me.'*

Oh, I'll do better than that. I arrived just as the cleaner was leaving.

'Good grief what happened to you?'

'Incredible I know, but I was attacked last night, by a bloody huge bird, an Owl I think. Spent four hours in 'A and E'. Eleven stitches in my head, three on my face and seven in my hand.'

'Oh I believe you. Why wouldn't I? Where did it happen?'

The silence tells me you're fumbling for lies.

'Decided to take the shortcut to the pub, went through the park. The thing just swooped at me screeching, gouging me and beating me with its wings. Look at the bruises.'

'They can be very territorial, Owls. Tawnys in particular, don't like anyone on their patch. She's made her point by the looks of things.'

The Darkening Season

I watch you steal a glance at the diamond ring, the one you tried to take, your eyes darting here and there telling me confusion was taking hold.

'Anyway must dash. Locksmiths due this afternoon. Lost one of my keys and well, you can't be too careful can you? I mean, anyone could just walk in, snoop around, rummage through your personal belongings, take whatever.'

I fix my gaze on the diamond ring, deliberately spinning it around my finger hoping your thoughts are heading beyond reason.

'I trust they cleaned those gashes properly?'

'Yeah I got antibiotics. Said they'd never seen anything like it. An Owl attacking so aggressively.'

'Penicillin, very wise! Look, maybe this is the wrong time but I don't think we should see each other again. I suppose I'm a bit of an Owl myself really. Solitary, territorial. Relationships are not really my thing. Oh, for the record, they will attack, if provoked. It's very rare, but they are birds of prey after all. You know, Folklore has it that the Owl, being a creature of keen sight, can often unmask a deceiver.'

'Anyhow, Toodle Pip.'

The Darkening Season

Graveyard Guardian

Druids honour all Nature especially Trees. Our Celtic ancestors had a deep connection with Trees and taught us that each Tree is a Being, an incarnation of wisdom, with its own unique medicine and gifts. The death defying, evergreen Yew has the reputation as the tree of eternal life. The Yew grows in a very unique way, regenerating with such remarkable continuity that many live for more than a thousand years. For our Druid ancestors and modern day Druids the Yew symbolizes many things in particular, immortality, death and rebirth. For this many were planted on ancient Pagan temple sites. The Druid belief in reincarnation led to Graves being dug around the Yew, earning this remarkable ancient wonder the reputation as the 'Graveyard Tree' or 'Tree of the Dead.'

The Darkening Season

Wondrous Yew In graveyards kept by Ancient Magic
To resurrect from stony ground the wisdom of the long dead
Many moons and starlit skies, steadfast Yew wise, twists
Deadly branches heaven bound, roots buried deep in bony ground
Graveyard guardian, bringer of dreams, funeral tree speak to me
Tell of ancestors' old, their secrets bestowed, whisperings
In the pitch of night, from souls who rest above the skies,
As I lay here beneath you to rest my eyes.

Saille

The Darkening Season

The Darkening Season

Alyson Faye

Originally I trained as a teacher/tutor who wrote children's books/poetry as a hobby. Collins Educational published my novel for children, 'Soldiers in the Mist' in 1996. Fast forward to 2016 I now live near Bronte terrain in West Yorkshire with my partner, teen son and 3 rescue cats. I write mainly noir Flash Fiction which is available to read on line at sites including TubeFlash/The Casket of Fictional Delights/AD HOC/Three Drops from a Cauldron and Horror Tree. My collection 'Badlands' is coming out with indie publisher Chapel Town Books later in 2017. I have several short stories available to download on www.alfiedog.com and www.etherbooks.com My latest children's book 'The Runaway Umbrella' is out on amazon Kindle. I have a ghost story collection coming out in December 2017 which includes the prize winning gothic horror story, 'Mother Love', also published in 'Women in Horror Annual 2'

Apart from writing, I enjoy singing, swimming, crafting and eating chocolate.

My blog is at www.alysonfayewordpress.wordpress.com

The Darkening Season

All Hallow's Eve

We gorge ourselves on the scents and sounds of the street market. On every stall rows of pumpkin heads leer at us, pyramids of witches' hats threaten to topple over, a skeleton busker dances a jig, whilst in amongst the crowds tiny ghouls and demons run around. We smile indulgently at their antics. They are so innocent, so…. unaware.

From behind the church walls we hear the notes of a lone pipe. Lured over, we make our way through the long grasses entwining round the tombstones. Among them skinny black shadows flit.

You tug at my hand. You are so eager to join them. I grip your hand tightly. A sob fills my chest.

A bedraggled child steps forward. She's unkempt and filthy with huge dark eyes. She's so thin you can see the fading daylight through her. She beckons and ventures a small, pitiful smile, showing rotted teeth and a glimpse of a black tongue.

The Darkening Season

Repelled I step away from her, but you do not. Instead you reach out and take the girl's bony hand. The pipe's music soars to a crescendo and I know you cannot resist. Not on this night. When the dead roam and come a-calling. I have to let you go. It is time.

Selfishly, I have kept you with me. You have been chained by my love. By my desire to hold on.

I watch you drift away, joining and blending into the shadow crowd.

You will always be my soul mate. My own Eve.

The Darkening Season

Willow Web

The night light emitted a tiny glow. Inside the clew of silk worms toiled ceaselessly. However to no avail since the shadow creeping across Lizzy's bedroom wall swallowed up all their light. Lizzy, lay wide awake, huddled under the covers. What would the shadow visitor take from her tonight? Last night it had stolen her toes. The night before her laugher. She had managed to hide these thefts from her mum by keeping her shoes on all day and not making any jokes.

Giant shadow fingers stretched out towards her bed. They were as thick as tar but not sticky. The bed covers wafted up and the spindly shadows fingers stroked Lizzy's face then outlined her lips. Lizzy lay frozen and shuddering. Unable to fight back.

Next morning Lizzy couldn't speak. Not a word. Her mum found her cowering behind the door when she came in to wake her up. At once she spotted black spores clinging to the wallpaper. She understood immediately what had been happening.

"Don't be afraid. I can help you my love." She gave Lizzy a huge hug.

The Darkening Season

Next she foraged a huge vanilla scented drawing pad from her seemingly bottomless bag and a twiggy bunch of charcoal sticks.

"Draw what you saw my love," she instructed, her voice gruff with anger. Lizzy obeyed. Her fingers flew over the thick paper, deftly sketching the huge shadow's outline with its elongated limbs.

Her mum watched her closely then nodded, "I thought as much." She swallowed hard. "We call it the Shadow Thief. It's an ancient creature. Still clinging onto life in this century. It is most powerful at this time of year when All Hallow's Eve draws nigh. This is when the veil is thinnest between the worlds of the living and the dead. They cross over to steal parts of children for their own uses. They need your voice to talk in their world. They need your laughter to feel joy. They are cannibals."

Lizzy felt a surge of relief at hearing her mum's explanation. It was not all in her head as she had feared. She never questioned how her mother knew about such things. She was not like the other mothers at the school gates, who scrabbled at their iPhones, who gossiped like squawking gulls, who baked immaculate cakes, who went to the gym and got manicures.

True her mum did make a lot of stuff at home. Some of her creations were up for sale on 'Etsy', but there were others which most definitely were never to be shown off. It had been this way for as long as Lizzy could remember. Just her, her mum and the secrets. The willow web was one of these.

At dawn the next morning mother and daughter set out to harvest the wood from the willows clinging to the river banks. The wood was dew soaked and really bendy. At home Lizzy's mum sat at their kitchen table, fixed her black framed spectacles across her nose and firmly grasped the willow wands, weaving them dexterously into an intricate web.

While her fingers worked, she chanted. Lizzy listening could pick out certain words: "bio abrancar banastra tona menino."*

She sensed the power of these ancient words and let them calm her.

"It will help to bind the willow and make it strong. We need just two more ingredients to finish. First a mirror which has seen and stored your image in its memory."

Lizzy went upstairs and brought down her hand mirror. Her mum smashed the glass carefully into a bowl. The tiny shards glimmered, reflecting Lizzy's face back at her. It was all broken and shattered.

'That's how I feel on the inside too,' Lizzy thought.

"Now we must weave the glass pieces into the web." Her mum's fingers flew, carefully securing the shards to the willow. The web glittered in the sunshine creating myriad rainbows.

Lizzy wrote, 'Beautiful,' on her pad but she couldn't move her face into a smile.

Her mum squeezed her shoulder, "Not long now Lizzy my love. It's nearly over."

She opened the fridge door and pulled out a container filled with brown rusty fluid. She always joked that it was her 'secret stash.' Lizzy shuddered, knowing what the liquid was.

Plucking the hair ribbon from Lizzy's head, her mum dip-dyed it in the brown liquid. The pigs' blood slowly stained the blue ribbon, which had strands of Lizzy's fair hair clinging to it.

"Yuk!" Lizzy mouthed.

Her mum laughed, "You won't be saying that later. You'll be grateful I'm doing this."

The Darkening Season

Next she wrapped the blood stained ribbon around the willow web.

"There. It is done. We'll let it dry and then we'll hang it in your bedroom window tonight."

Outside in the street, candlelit pumpkin heads were appearing in the neighbours' windows and Lizzy watched the local children set off in groups, dressed up as witches, wizards, ghouls and goblins. Outside she sensed the excitement and anticipation. However no one came knocking to 'trick or treat' at their door. They never did. The neighbours were polite enough but kept their distance.

Lizzy wasn't sure exactly why. She and her mum had done nothing wrong. But some primal instinct warned the neighbours that the two women were not of their breed. The separateness made Lizzy sad but it had always been that way. At least now their kind were not burned or drowned. 'There had been some progress over the centuries,' she thought.

At bedtime Lizzy snuggled under her duvet, while her mum perched cross-legged on a Harry Potter beanbag. The willow web was tied in place across the bedroom window. It hung though waiting for a giant spider to make it home.

"I'll read you a story to help pass the time Lizzy."

Her mum picked up their battered copy of 'Grimm's Fairy Tales', which had been handed down from mother to daughter for generations. The pages were foxed and familiar. Lizzy loved their musty smell.

Lizzy listened to her mum's soothing voice and watched her lunar clock tick off the minutes. She drifted off to sleep but awoke with a start. Glancing at the clock, she saw it was midnight already. Panicking she jerked upright, but her mum lightly touched

The Darkening Season

her shoulder and whispering "Shush," pointed towards the window.

The willow web was stretching inwards, creaking and bending but holding firm. Lizzy gasped in fear. Behind it a shadowy figure was pushing hard to gain entry. Its long black inky arms were reaching through the web, while its skinny spindly legs were pressed against the window frame for purchase. The web did not split. The shadow thief scrabbled frantically at the willow and Lizzy heard the glass shards tinkle, as if the web was answering back. The shadow thief bent its huge elongated snout to sniff the blood soaked ribbon and then extended its long black tongue to taste it. It recoiled, unpeeled all of its limbs at speed from the window frame and clambered swiftly upwards to to the roof. They heard its terrible feet skittering away over the tiles.

"Get thee gone yonder Shadow Thief. You will take nothing more from my child." Her mum spoke out clearly.

Crack! The window pane shattered into a crazy jigsaw, but still the web held firm. Lizzy felt something rising up in her throat. She gagged, once, twice, then she spat out blobs of gunky black spittle onto the long suffering carpet. They lay there wriggling like worms. Her mum bent down with a lit candle touching the flame to the worms. They reared up, then sizzled into ash. Lizzy watched horrified but fascinated.

"Mum thank you!" Lizzy cried and threw her arms around her. She wriggled her newly restored toes and felt joy fill her heart. She was remade; she was returned. She was whole again.

(The idea for this longer piece originated from a drabble called 'Shadow Thief' which was published on www.thedrabblewordpress.com)

The Darkening Season

*brio- might/power
abrancar -to embrace
banastra- basket
tona -skin/bark/scum of milk
menino -kid/child
(These are all Galician words of Celtic origin)

The Darkening Season

Zombie Hunting

This is not what I had in mind when Lisa had said we should dress up for Halloween and make a night of it. I'd been thinking more along the lines of matching witch and wizard costumes, a pub crawl, getting hammered and going back to mine.

Crouching in the middle of bloody Dalby Forest in a hide, all weaponed up, decked out in camouflage gear – none of this was what I'd bargained for. I'm freezing, fed up and sober. Outside it's pitch black. The silence is broken by occasional howls and screams.

"Let's do something different." Lisa had suggested. "It'll be a fun bonding thing. We can spend Halloween fighting side by side like in 'The Walking Dead.'" She'd made me watch season after season of that telly show.

I'd never heard of 'Zombie Hunting'. However it's a real money spinner. Halloween's the biggest night of the year for the companies who offer this event. OK it's only paint balls and dress up but the photographs on the 'ZombiesRUs' website look realistically horrifying. The gear you get to hunt with is pretty cool too.

The Darkening Season

"Time to go shoot. Let's get out there!" Lisa shouts out, as she stands up with her right arm raised. Reluctantly I follow her. I have to. We're on the deluxe couples' package.

It's pretty creepy at night out in the woods. I'm jumping at shadows like a kid whilst holding my semi automatic paint gun in front of me like a shield. My heart is hammering away.

A figure comes streaking out of the darkness, wailing. It's covered in white body paint, has a bloodstained mouth and is moving fast. Very fast. Not like a human. I have a flashback to the film 'World War Z' and feel my adrenaline levels roar upwards. I also feel a bit sick.

Lisa gets off a few shots and the 'zombie' collapses, writhing impressively. His chest erupting in crimson paint sprays, some of which rain onto my girlfriend.

"Awesome!" She air punches and wipes her face. I eye her with respect. This is a new side to my Lisa. Zombie killer.

Me on the other hand -well I'm sweating, my mouth's dry as dust and I just want to climb a tree. But shoulder to shoulder, we march on through the bushes, shoving through the undergrowth.

I am awash with emotions, mainly fear but there's love in there too. Overcome by everything, I whisper to Lisa, "I love you. You know that don't you?" At that moment I don't doubt it one iota.

Lisa glances at me, with eyes like a pandas, however she looks pleased. "Mm do you? Well I…."

I'm destined never to find out what she going to say next, for a zombie bursts unheralded from behind a gnarly tree. He's carrying a huge axe, and shrieking. He's all white face, blue lips and rotting flesh.

The Darkening Season

Panicking, I grab Lisa and shove her in front of me as an offering.

"Take her!" I yell.

The zombie freezes. He lowers his axe. "Bloody hell mate. That's a bit off in nit?" He has a broad Yorkshire accent.

Lisa bursts into tears and the zombie puts his arm round her shaking shoulders. "C'mon love. You come with me and we'll go get a cuppa."

I watch my ex girlfriend in her camo gear walk off into the greenery with the zombie towering protectively over her.

(A shorter version of this piece has been published on http://www.postcardshorts.com)

The Darkening Season

James Nash

James Nash is writer and a poet. A long-term resident of Leeds, his third collection of poems, 'Coma Songs' was published in 2003 and reprinted in 2006. He has two poems in 'Branch-Lines' [Enitharmon Press 2007] among fifty contemporary poets, including Seamus Heaney and U. A. Fanthorpe.

In 2012 his selected poems 'A Bit of An Ice Breaker' and a five-star collection, 'Some Things Matter', were published by Valley Press, followed in 2015 by 'Cinema Stories' written with fellow poet Matthew Hedley Stoppard.

www.jamesnash.co.uk

The Darkening Season

A Sonnet

When I glimpse the sea down across the fields
To my left, [I'd thought it would be my right]
My blood beats faster as the morning yields
Up its hope, scatters the shadows of night.
Apart from meadows and sky I'm alone,
But they breathe as I breathe, promise me,
While chalk gleams on the banks like bone,
A part in the world and yet still be free.
Now as my bike bounces back down the lane
Towards where the sea and land are one,
The wheat glitters with harvest gold again
My spirit and the landscape are as one.
Brief these moments, blessed in what they bring,
In this belonging, which is everything.

Aubade

Waking slowly, I look
through the window
at the silver sky and fields of frost,
reflections of each other,
where nothing moves
where lines of wall and hedge converge,
and at their corners
large trees see out the final,
chilly disciplines of their watch.
I carefully clasp my mug of tea
as if it holds your heartbeat
your dreaming breath.

A dog barks on a nearby farm,
the sky becomes the faintest blue,
and cattle move stiffly
out of a frozen enchantment.
The machinery of morning is starting up,
and I stand there, considering,
trying
to trace
your sleeping outline in the hills.

Towpath

I'm racing to beat the twilight
as it hangs itself like damp washing
in the trees
and the swans on the water
float whiter than at any other time.
My wheels bump and whirr a commentary
on my journey into night
and one star gleams
over the abbey's ragged walls.

I'm racing to beat the twilight
alone
except for the last fisherman
packing up his rods and gear;
next week the year slips a cog
and changes
and he falls away behind me
into the gathering dusk.

I'm racing to beat the twilight
and as it darkens
naked men and women
seem to march
Around me in slow columns.
I see
their glazed flesh,
upper bodies catching the remaining light,
lips and nipples

The Darkening Season

dark flowers
frozen in the bud.
I hear
The sighing wind-band of their breathing,
The soft percussion of their feet.
My light bobs its beam ahead,
Illuminating
the remaining path.

The Darkening Season

Autumn

My hands are bark and twigs,
while warm flesh and muscle
glove your fingers.
I can feel the pulse,
the summer movement of blood through
the root of your thumb,
see it beneath your skin.

We stand in an open doorway,
while outside
leaves like rusty terriers tumble
under white boned birches,
quarrelling at their tips,
and bushes are clotted with
crimson berries and scarlet hips.

And through the pewter of an autumn sky.
in a temporary torch-beam of sunshine
I see fruit, like yellow light bulbs,
amongst the half-stripped silver leaves
of an apple tree, nearly over.

But you have to go.

Stay a moment more with me,
warming my hands in yours,
before, howling, I blow into winter.

The Darkening Season

John Ellis

I recently retired after a long career teaching English in schools and further education colleges. This has given me more time to focus on writing which has long been an interest and I joined the Otley Courthouse writers' group in April this year; this has been a great experience. I write in a variety of genres and for a variety of audiences including children's stories, ghost stories and poems.

My main focus at the moment is detective fiction and I have completed two novels of a projected series mostly set in the varied places and landscapes of Yorkshire. I have also written a work of "faction" about the extraordinary life of my Irish mother-in-law and my wife's "secret" half-brother. Like most writers I aspire to getting my writing published although I have discovered that this can be a long and tricky business!

The Darkening Season

Catoptrophobia

(fear of mirrors)

Anne was afraid of looking into mirrors. It wasn't that she didn't like her own face, her hair or her teeth. No. She was afraid of the figures she saw behind her; figures that stood still and expressionless, looking at her.

She often saw her mother and lots of her old relatives. There was also a man she didn't recognise who had a moustache and was dressed in very old-fashioned clothes. Then she saw him in an old family photograph. It was her great grandfather. All the people she saw had one thing in common: they were dead.

She'd been seeing these figures for a long time. At first when she was quite young it had been puzzling to her, especially when she asked her mother about the figures and her mother couldn't see anything and told her it was her imagination. Her father couldn't see anything either. Then it became quite cool to

The Darkening Season

see her secret people as she called them; something which it appeared no-one else could do.

But over the years, the whole thing had become much more disturbing. Now dead people whom she'd known and been close to, started to appear: her mother, a friend who'd been killed in an accident. This could have been consoling, but the way they appeared in the mirror with blank expressions made them seem lifeless, ghosts of the people she'd known. After years of keeping it all a secret, she didn't feel capable anymore of sharing it with anyone. She'd not told her partner.

One morning she glanced at the large hall mirror before leaving the house. The figures gathered there all slowly raised their arm to her as if in greeting. None of them had ever made any kind of movement before. She went out quickly and hurried down the street. She was too shocked and disturbed to concentrate on what she was doing and wandered across the road without looking.

Anne saw her partner when he arrived home in the early evening. He'd been crying and looked terrible. She gazed at him mournfully as he looked towards her. Unfortunately, he could never see her. He lacked Anne's unique ability.

The Darkening Season

Close the Barn Door

"Close the barn door Matthew!" shouted the farmer. "We don't want the animals in there."

The young farmhand who was walking towards the farmhouse, turned and looked back at the big barn where hay was stored for the winter. He was puzzled.

"I've just closed it!" he called back.

"How can you have? It's wide open."

Matthew shrugged his shoulders and walked back to the large wooden door and saw that the farmer was right. It was open. How could it be? The latch must have sprung open somehow. Swinging it closed again, he made absolutely sure that the metal latch was down and he shook the door to make certain it was secure.

While they were having lunch in the farmhouse, the farmer gave Matthew a lecture, pointing at him with his knife while he was eating.

The Darkening Season

"Keep your mind on what you're doing. It'll be haymaking soon; if you start day dreaming while we're using machinery, there'll be an accident"

Matthew ate in silence feeling a sense of injustice, but knew that it was no good arguing with the farmer. He could have sworn that door was shut.

In the afternoon, Matthew worked down at the bottom fields repairing a fence. The farmer stayed at the farm buildings tending to the animals. It was an overcast day which seemed to reflect his mood. The farm was not doing well and it would be a struggle to make ends meet financially by the end of the year. There was a strange tension in the atmosphere which he didn't like and the animals sensed it too. They were jumpy and hard to handle. Milk yields from the cows were down.

It was partly this mood which had made him snap at Matthew and he felt sorry for the lad now. By coincidence, just as he was thinking about this, he turned a corner into the yard to find his way blocked. The barn door was wide open. Not Matthew again? But no, not this time. Matthew was down in the fields and he'd been in the barn himself to get a rake. And he was sure that he'd closed the door when he left. He grasped the handle feelin exasperated, but as he pulled the door closed, it seemed like a wave of hot air coming from the inside of the barn blew over him. It was very odd as the day was cool and very little sun ever got into the barn even on sunny days. He walked off towards the cowshed to start the milking, feeling rather groggy and he never seemed to recover for the rest of the day.

The weather improved in the next few days and soon the hay was ready to be cut. Matthew and the other farmhands were working in the field next to the barn piling hay into haycocks to dry. In the middle of the afternoon, he started to feel strange. He

The Darkening Season

was thinking all the time about the barn and constantly towards it. He was convinced that something was happening in there and then he thought he saw smoke.

"Look out!" One of the other workers shouted to Matthew as the farmer drove past in the big tractor pulling the mower. Matthew jumped aside and then ran over to the barn. As he reached it he saw that, yet again, the door was open. He felt a compulsive curiosity but also a sense of fear about what he might find inside. Everything seemed to slow down; as he got to the door it opened a little wider, creaking as it did so. He went in slowly, his legs feeling weak. Inside it was gloomy and he could see very little as his eyes adjusted. It all seemed bigger than normal; he could just make out the wooden joists high above his head.

Everything seemed quiet, but then he heard a rustling noise on one side of barn where the first of the winter hay had been piled. He peered through the gloom; surely there was a shape there, a person? It moved and next to it was a small light which seemed to be growing. It was a fire; the barn was hot and airless, he had to get out! In a panic he ran back to the door, but everything seemed to slow down again. As in a nightmare, he couldn't get to the door fast enough and to his horror he saw that it was slowly closing. He knew he had to get out before the door closed or something terrible would happen. He thought he could hear a voice laughing faintly, but echoing all around the barn. With a violent effort he threw himself at what remained of the opening and just managed to fall rather than walk through before the door closed.

He lay panting on the ground for several minutes and shaking with shock. Then he heard the sound of footsteps running and the farmer and two of his men arrived. They forced the door open and there were shouts of

The Darkening Season

"Fire! Get some water in those buckets!"

Matthew was taken to the farmhouse to lie down on a bed. Here he continued to shake so a doctor was called. By the time he arrived, Matthew had calmed down sufficiently to explain what had happened. Luckily the doctor, a local man was not only sympathetic, but also had an extensive knowledge of local history.

"So this happened in the old barn did it?"

"Yes."

"Hm." the doctor looked thoughtful. "The old barn on Low Rakes Farm. I'm sure I've read about that old barn here. I'll look it up for you. I've got a feeling that strange things have happened before"

As Matthew was clearly on the mend the doctor didn't prescribe anything, but advised him to rest for a couple of days at the farmhouse where the farmer's wife would look after him and then left, promising to return in a few days' time. Matthew was left wondering what to make of it all. The farmer came up to the bedroom and told him they'd put out a small fire in the barn and asked him what he'd seen. The farmer clearly thought that he'd disturbed an intruder, but Matthew was not convinced

However it wasn't long before he felt completely recovered and returned to work and to his room in the farm cottage. There were no more incidents although he kept clear of the barn. Several days later he awoke in the night with the same feeling of dread which he had experienced on that afternoon. He went to his bedroom window and looked out. There was a full moon and the sky was clear. His bedroom window faced across the farmyard and he could see that, yet again, the barn door was open. At the same time the farmer also awoke, feeling that something was wrong. From his window he could also see the open door and he knew that he had secured it himself that evening as one of his last jobs of the day. As he watched, a shadowy figure appeared and went into the barn.

Furious, the farmer pulled on his clothes and ran down the stairs. Someone was trespassing and they could only be up to no good at this time of night. He was going to put a stop to all this trouble with the barn. He grabbed his shotgun and a torch and walked stealthily across the yard, intending to catch the intruder in the act. When he got to the door he could hear what seemed to be a person laughing, but the noise was strange and echoing as if it was coming from a great distance. As he entered the barn, hot air struck his face but he was too angry to register surprise. In the middle of the barn a figure was standing with his back to the farmer. The barn door slammed shut. The farmer raised his gun in his right hand and grasped the torch in his left.

"Right!" he shouted. "Turn round and tell me what you're doing in my barn!"

There was more echoing laughter. "So you think it's funny do you? You're setting fires off in here; turn round or I'll give you a blast of this."

Slowly the figure turned round and the farmer shone his torch at the head. He shrieked with horror and dropped the torch. The face had no features, only a twisted, grinning mouth; everything else seemed to have been burned away. As the farmer ran for the door, flames leaped up all around him and the barn quickly became an inferno. Like Matthew he felt that everything slowed down. With a tremendous effort, he made it to the door, but it was shut. He pulled and kicked at it, but it wouldn't move. A hand fell on his shoulder.

From his window, Matthew saw the farmer go into the barn and then heard his cry. He rushed out and pelted across the yard. He pulled at the barn door which opened easily from the outside.

The Darkening Season

Smoke billowed out and he could hear the crackle of wood and hay burning. Coughing, he struggled in and could just make out the figure of the farmer lying on the floor. He grasped him under the arms and dragged him to the door. Just as he succeeded in getting the body clear of the barn, the burning roof collapsed with a tremendous crash. Matthew sank to the floor exhausted as he heard voices shouting and people running towards him.

Three days later, the doctor arrived at the farm to visit the farmer who was making a good recovery. Matthew had saved his life. He passed a group of workmen who had demolished what remained of the barn and were now breaking up the foundations. Matthew was just coming into the farmhouse. It was the first time the doctor had seen him since the fateful night.

"Ah, the hero of the hour. Well done young man!"

Matthew grinned and looked embarrassed. "I have something for you here," the doctor continued, and he produced a very old, musty smelling book. "This is a chronicle of this area written in the nineteenth century by a local squire. It's a very interesting source of information about those times. Now, take a look at this." He opened the book and pointed to a paragraph. Matthew found the Victorian writing difficult to read, so the doctor read an entry for 1843.

"3rd July. On this day a terrible fire at Low Rakes Farm. Thomas Whitkirk found burned to death. This is the judgement of his Maker."

"What does that last bit mean: "The judgement of his Maker"?"

"I'm not exactly sure but it could mean that he'd started the fire, but got caught in it himself."

"But why would he do that?"

The Darkening Season

"I suspect he may have had a grudge against someone. Maybe he'd been sacked from his job on the farm and wanted to get revenge. There's a record of him working here. The interesting thing is the date: 3rd July."

"Yes, it was 3rd July on the night of the fire here too, so that's the second time that barn's been burned down on 3rd July; seems an amazing coincidence."

The doctor looked thoughtful

"I wonder if it is."

"Hey! Come over here; look at this!"

Their conversation was interrupted by one of the workmen calling them over to the site of the barn. A group of men were gathered around a hole they had discovered. In the bottom were the charred remains of a human skeleton.

The Darkening Season

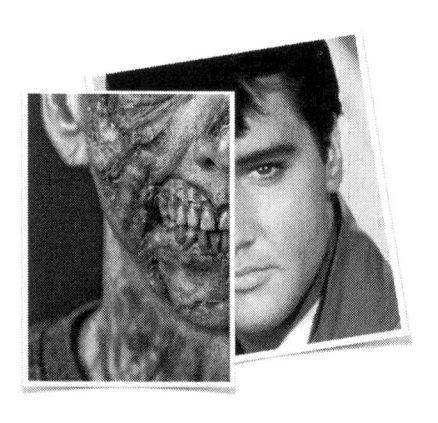

"Love Me Tender"

The car was dead; it could go no further that night. He got out, pulled up his hood and looked up and down the road. It was dark and foggy. He could see no lights in the distance to guide him, though he knew there were some small towns in the bottom of this steep sided Yorkshire valley. He got out his phone, but the battery was lifeless. He didn't want to stay in the car, but he knew that walking off aimlessly could be dangerous. The fields and moors swelled up for miles and to get lost in the cold and wet could be fatal.

He slammed the door and strode up the road with determination. He'd been up this way before and he was fairly sure that if he kept going for a little way, there were some tracks up from the road to farmhouses. This was his main hope of finding shelter for the night and help.

He trudged on through the foggy drizzle, pulling his coat tight around him. No cars passed, but an owl swooped low and silently over the road and then perched on the damp wall staring at him. After a quarter of a mile, he was relieved to see a track leaving the road and presumably travelling up the hillside. A weathered wooden sign announced High Moor Farm. The track went off into utter blackness and he could see no comforting distant light. It was not an inviting prospect, but he decided that it was his best option. He had to go up to that house.

The bumpy, unsurfaced track twisted and turned up the fields and through gates before at last he was able to make out a glow of light. He headed towards this and was rewarded when suddenly a dark building loomed up and he could make out the light of a single bare bulb shining in a narrow stone porch. There was a large heavy looking van, its bodywork, bumped and scraped, parked outside some old stables. He glanced quickly inside the cab.

He felt some relief that he'd finally made it and knocked on the door. He looked at his watch: 1.00am. Would anyone be awake at this time? Would anyone hear his knocking? He stood waiting and shivering. There was something unpleasant about this place. It was gloomy and ramshackle with paint peeling off the window frames. The curtains were ragged and there was no light visible inside. If it hadn't been for the van which had left recent tyre marks he would have thought the place was uninhabited.

He knocked again and finally heard footsteps inside. A bolt was drawn back, a lock turned and the door creaked open. A ferocious looking face with a scar down one side peered out. The man held a shot gun in his muscular arms. The traveller noticed he was fully dressed; he had not been raised from his bed.

"What the bloody hell do you want at this time of night?" the big man snarled.

"My car's bust; it's down on the road. It's too late to go anywhere. Can I just stay inside here until morning? I'll just sleep on the floor, anywhere. It's Mr Westwood isn't it?"

The Darkening Season

The big man's eyes narrowed in suspicion. He looked ready to slam the door in the traveller's face.

"How do you know my name? What are you after? I'm the farmer here; this is my land." He raised the shotgun.

"I saw your name on something in the cab of that van out there. Please; I've got nowhere to go. I'm cold and wet."

The farmer lowered the shot gun and looked at the pale face and vacant eyes beneath the hood. The man looked exhausted and ill. Normally he was a hard man not given to doing favours, but for some reason he couldn't bring himself to turn this character out.

"OK you can stay 'till it gets light, but no funny business. If this is some kind of trick then look out." He raised the gun again.

"I'm not a robber; I'm just a bloke in trouble."

The farmer grunted and then smiled to himself; an idea had come to him for a bit of what he thought of as fun.

"Well you just go in this room down here and stay there." He led the traveller along a dark passage until they reached a door at the end which he opened and beckoned him in. "Maybe I'll see you in the morning and maybe not. Not everyone finds this house, shall we say, peaceful." The traveller entered the dark room. "I hope you like your companions," said the farmer and he shut the door. A sinister laugh could be heard as he retreated down the passage.

Companions? What did he mean? thought the traveller as he fumbled for a light switch in the dark room. He groped around, fell over a chair and then crashed into a standard lamp. He felt the lamp for a switch, found it and clicked. Unexpectedly the light came on and he was immediately startled: the head of a bear was staring at him, a massive creature ferociously baring its teeth. It was about to leap on him! Then he realised its animation was staged; the animal was dead and stuffed though still an impressive full-sized beast. He looked around the room and saw that it was full of similarly preserved specimens mostly predators: wolves, foxes, stoats, some in glass cases and all looking terrifying with bared teeth. The taxidermy had achieved such a high standard of realism that it was almost impossible to believe that they were dead and not about to attack. Surely there was saliva glistening in their mouths and wasn't there some slight movements at times? Presumably this is what his unfriendly host meant by "companions."

Besides the unnerving array of stuffed creatures arranged around the room there was a large bookcase stacked with ancient looking hard backed volumes. He scanned these and discovered a number of titles concerning the art of taxidermy and others contained wildlife photographs but of an old and rather poor quality. Clearly someone who'd lived here in the past had developed an interest and considerable skill in this rather strange practice, but who? Then he noticed some smaller volumes each marked "Journal" with various volume numbers. He took one of these down and opened it. On the first page was written "Taxidermy Journal of Charles Westwood 1896- 7." Clearly this was the work of the creator of his "companions."

The room also contained two large armchairs and the traveller, having satisfied himself that there was nothing actually alive and threatening in the room with him, sat down in one these and flicked through the pages hoping that it might contain some interesting information about the man and his methods. He didn't manage to read much before tiredness overcame him. He turned off the light and slumped down in the chair.

The Darkening Season

He looked a forlorn and exhausted figure still wearing his hood. It was dark and claustrophobic with curtains drawn tight across the windows. There was silence apart from occasional creaks. He tried to locate where these were coming from and decided it must be from the stuffed creatures. Once or twice he switched the light back on and it seemed that some of the animals had moved slightly from their original positions, but however long he stared nothing happened so it must have been in his imagination. He managed to get reasonably comfortable in the chair and began to think about his host as he sat there dozing. He was just the kind of man he'd expected to find in an isolated place like this, but did anyone else live here?

Sometime later he heard another sound and opened his eyes. This time he'd left the light on. Nothing had changed, although maybe that stuffed wolf somehow seemed a little closer to him. Then he realised the sound was outside. It was a voice singing:

Love me tender
Love me sweet
Never let me go

He recognised the song; he went to the window and pulled back the curtain. It was very dark and foggy, but there was a face just outside the window. It was a woman's face. Her eyes were lifeless, but they stared at him. Her face and hair were smeared with blood and she held her head at a peculiar angle. As he stared back at her, her lips parted to reveal a mouth full of blood and broken teeth. She began to sing again:

The Darkening Season

Love me tender
Love me true
All my dreams fulfilled

The fog continued to thicken and settle around the old farmhouse. The silence was intense. The sound of no living thing could be heard. When dawn came it brought no light to the hillside.

At seven o'clock in the morning, the farmer got out of bed cursing and swearing. He was late for milking the cows. He'd stayed up too late the previous night, drinking cans of lager, playing poker games online and losing money in the process. His gambling and drinking had destroyed his marriage and now he had to do everything on the farm by himself.

He scratched his dirty beard as he came downstairs and suddenly remembered his late night visitor. He smiled; how had he got on in the Animal Room as he called it? It was a spooky old place into which he went as rarely as possible, but somehow he daren't get rid of all the creepy stuffed animals his great, great uncle had made years ago. There were family superstitions about those specimens: bad luck or worse would befall anyone who tampered with them. There were rumours that the old boy had used some secret methods of preservation involving the dark arts which rendered the stuffed animals so lifelike that they actually could come back to life at times. He didn't believe in any of that but nevertheless he didn't feel he could disturb them. Just his bad luck to be lumbered with them all.

As he entered his untidy kitchen and closed the door behind him he was surprised to see his guest already up and looking out of the window at the continuing foggy weather. He was still wearing his hood up.

The Darkening Season

"Oh I see you're up then; found the kitchen. How did you find your accommodation?" He smiled wickedly. The traveller turned; his flat expression was exactly the same as the previous night.

"Fine. My stay here has been very satisfactory. I have confirmed what I suspected. I knew it from the moment I saw your van. Those marks and bulges on the side. It got those in a crash didn't it?"

The farmer was open mouthed in astonishment.

"What? How did you...? What's it got to do with you anyway?"

The traveller went on; his pale face never changed and his voice conveyed no emotion, but the eyes were suddenly extremely menacing. The farmer took a step back.

"I was in the car you smashed into the side of trying to overtake on that corner on the road back there. It was exactly a year ago last night; but I'm sure you've forgotten that. You pushed my car into the wall and then it rolled completely over. You never stopped did you? Though you knew what had happened. You were drunk weren't you? That's why. And you got away with it because there were no witnesses. I bet you told the police some lies about the damage to your van, if they ever came up here at all. Anyway, I had an idea you probably lived nearby and thought you owned that stretch of road. It was in the crash that this happened."

Abruptly he pulled back his hood and the horrified farmer saw that a whole section of his head was missing.

"No!" he cried. He turned round and tried to open the door out of the kitchen but the handle wouldn't move.

"That wasn't the worst," continued the traveller in the same level, emotionless voice. "You see, my partner was with me. Her face was smashed in and her neck broken while my brains were being dashed out. We'd been out for the evening and were driving home. We were listening to some music. We like some of the old Elvis songs. The CD was still playing when the police and ambulance arrived too late to do anything. Shall I sing one to you? The one that was playing when you killed us?"

The farmer saw that he was holding a metal fire poker which he must have found in the old hearth in the Animal Room.

"She was here last night," continued the traveller, "singing to remind me what I had to do:

Love me tender
Love me true"

Suddenly he raised the metal bar and moved towards the terrified farmer with a speed which was not human.

The body was found some days later with severe injuries to the head and face. The neck was broken. There were no signs that anyone other than the victim had been in or around the farmhouse and no vehicles were parked in the vicinity. There was a strange, dusty room with a lot of antique stuffed animals, but the dust was thick on all the chairs and surfaces and the police concluded that no-one had been in there for months. The only unusual thing they found was a curious note left near the body containing the words:

You have made
My life complete
And I love you so.

The Darkening Season

The Ghost Trail

The Ghost Trail guide lounged against the wall under the imitation gas lamp and yawned. He looked contemptuously at his ridiculous outfit of black suit with tails and a top hat which made him look like a Victorian undertaker and reflected that he'd really had enough of this job. He couldn't face yet another boring trip around the sites supposedly frequented by the city's ghosts and ghoulies. Not that any of the ghosts really existed. It was all invented and elaborated to boost the city's income from tourism. How pathetic when you thought that people were prepared to pay £8 for the privilege of being trundled round the dark alleyways and rotting graveyards; along damp paths by the river and into the draughty marketplace! How they gazed at him open mouthed as he told them the grisly stories and how they oohd and aahd when he came to a dramatic moment. Using all his flair for melodrama, he hammed it up atrociously, but they seemed to love it and never seemed to notice when he went way over the top. How he despised them for being so credulous and gullible!

The Darkening Season

It was nearly seven o'clock. Just time for a cigarette before the party arrived. This was a group booking: even worse! He was seeing them at the fag end of their day. They would have been driven in by coach in the morning to spend all day trudging round the sights and shops and eating at McDonalds. Some would get tired on the ghost trip, start talking about their purchases and asking each other what time it was.

Exactly as the nearby church clock struck seven, he saw them walking slowly down the street towards him. He stood up and adjusted his long black cape and hat. What an absurd costume! Just like a refugee from some awful old Hammer horror film: Christopher Lee as Dracula on a bad day. He twirled his black cane, or was it a magician's wand and threw himself into the part.

"Roll up, Roll up!" he wanted to shout. "After your dose of Dickens in the Victorian Christmas market, come for some more hokum on the phoney ghost tour of the city's so- called haunted sites." But he didn't, mainly because the more authentic he made it sound, the more likely they were to tip him at the end.

The party drew near. It was a cold evening and they were all muffled up with hats, hoods, and scarves. It was so dark that he could not see any of their faces, but then he rarely could and preferred it that way. He didn't want to engage with people as he hammed up his role; it was too embarrassing.

"Ladies and gentlemen; welcome to the Ghost Trail. I trust that you are all aware of what lies before you. There is still time," he swished his cloak and moved to a place where a dim street lamp threw an eerie light onto his face, "to think again."

There was no response from his audience and his heart sank. This lot looked as if they were going to be hard work. Never mind, it would be a challenge. He liked that better than the silly people who screamed and clapped at everything. Let's see if I can get

The Darkening Season

them into the spirit; or at least frightened by the spirits. He chuckled to himself at his own joke.

"Very well everyone; follow me and keep close together!" he announced with a dramatic flourish.

He led the party away through a maze of dimly lit alleyways in the old part of the city until they came to a particularly dark passage. The guide slunk into the shadows.

"This passage is a dead end. There is no escape and it was here in 1837 that Molly Hanson, a serving girl at The White Bull ran to try to escape from her murderer. But of course there was no escape and she was stabbed to death. Since that terrible night long ago, many people have heard her footsteps running up this passage and her frantic screams as she realised there was no way out. Her body was found against that very wall which was blocking her way."

He suddenly produced a torch and shone it up the passage. "Just there at the top." All the heads followed the direction of the torchlight and they saw the figure of a woman lying up against the wall. Her neck appeared to be covered in red. This usually produced the first gasp of surprise or even a scream from the party, but on this occasion there appeared to be no reaction.

"Not to worry ladies and gentlemen, it's only a waxwork dummy."

He was quite proud of this trick and disappointed at the subdued reaction of his clients which amounted to nothing more than a fixed stare at the gruesome mannequin. Curiously, he was the one who felt a sense of eeriness in the atmosphere and he decided to move on quickly. He cast a final glance at the dummy and shuddered; the blood on the neck somehow seemed more realistic than usual.

The Darkening Season

The second stopping point was down a steep cobbled path to the river. The deep black water slid silently past, lapping at their feet.

"In 1751 a poor man called James Gibson lived not far from here. The story is that he lost all his money when his business failed. In a terrible moment of despair, he walked to a spot just a little further up from here. It was a dark December night very much like this and he threw himself into the water. Someone walking over the bridge downstream saw a shape passing underneath, but the body was never found. People still claim to see a body float past here and…"

The guide stopped abruptly as one of the party raised an arm and pointed towards the river. He looked and actually there was something going downstream, maybe a ragged piece of material which had been blown into the water. It was a macabre coincidence and he laughed it off.

"Well, there you are, even more lifelike than usual"

As there was no further reaction he moved on. He was beginning to wish that this tour was at an end. Whatever tricks he seemed to try, the actual circumstances were even spookier, but nothing seemed to move this lot.

He led them slowly back up from the river and through the dark streets to a gloomy looking church. He led them down a wet mossy path behind the black mass of the building to the graveyard behind. Here was a mass of gravestones of differing shapes and sizes.

The guide paused and looked at his watch. He had timed it perfectly. He walked a few paces amongst the stones and stood against a weathered cross.

"This graveyard may seem peaceful now, but in 1789 it was the scene of a very strange incident. At that time, as many of you will know, there was a great interest in dissecting the human body in order to advance the knowledge of human anatomy. It was quite common for bodies to be stolen from graveyards such as this and sold on to doctors. One winter's night, two men came to dig up a body from a newly dug grave near where I'm standing. As they approached, they saw a figure sitting on the stone. One of the men knew the woman who had recently died and when he got near he realised, to his horror that it was her, looking at them with a pale, vacant stare. Her long hair hung down her back. And so…"

He paused and looked around expectantly. At this point two figures were supposed to leap out from behind another gravestone dressed as eighteenth century grave robbers, giving the clients a fright as another part of the show. However, no-one had appeared except, he saw to his unease that there was a figure obviously female from her long hair, sitting on a grave stone not far away. She was too distant for any particular features to be made out; she was probably one of the city's sad homeless who often frequented churches and graveyards. As the guide turned his attention back to the people on the tour, he saw that yet again the impact of the story appeared to be nil.

And so it went on. However hard the guide tried, the group remained attentive but silent and apparently unmoved. No matter how macabre, bloody or ghastly the story was, no-one spoke or appeared to be affected in any way. On the other hand, strange and unaccountable things continued to happen so that by the time they arrived back at the starting point, the guide was exhausted, frustrated and puzzled. He was also angry with his two assistants who had failed to turn up to play their parts as the grave robbers. He brought the tour to an end and headed with relief for the company's little office. By the office door he saw the two actors talking; they were dressed in their grave snatcher costumes. One was looking at something on his phone. The guide strode over angrily.

"Where the hell have you been? I've had a terrible time with that lot."

"Which lot?" The two men looked at him.

"That last tour party; never got an ounce of response from them and then to make matters worse, you two never turned up at the graveyard."

"You can't mean the seven o'clock group?" one of them asked.

"Why not?"

"Haven't you heard?"

"What?"

"The news?"

"No I've heard nothing; I've been doing tours all day, no time for playing around reading the news. My phone battery's dead anyway."

The two actors looked at each other and one shook his head. The other looked hard at the guide

"There's been a terrible accident; the party you were supposed to be taking on the ghost trail at seven were all killed in a coach crash. Look."

He passed the phone to the guide who took it and read the headline:

"25 killed in Britain's worst coach crash for forty years."

Beneath this he read; "A coach carrying a party of tourists has crashed at The Devil's Bridge in the Yorkshire Dales, a notorious accident black spot. The brakes appear to have failed as the coach came down the steep hill to the hairpin bend. An eye witness said it smashed through the wall and plummeted into the ravine; when

The Darkening Season

it landed it caught fire. Police and emergency workers say there appears to be no survivors"

The guide was stunned. He looked up from the phone to see the actor looking at him curiously,

"When we found out what had happened, we didn't go to the graveyard. There was clearly not going to be a seven o'clock tour. So where have you been?"

The guide couldn't reply; he looked pale. He turned round to look for the party he had just taken around the City Ghost Trail, but there was no sign of anyone.

The Darkening Season

The Darkening Season

Cynthia Richardson

After a successful career in further education, Cynthia retired from her role as Bradford and District Learning Partnership Manager in 2012.

A friend encouraged her to take up writing as 'she always has a good tale to tell'.

Gathering on her varied life experiences, Cynthia has a passion for writing short stories.

Cynthia has two grown children and enjoys dog walking, looking for bargains and days out at the seaside.

The Darkening Season

Ghost in the Cafe

My eyes are red but I cry no more instead the weather mirrors my mood. The rain sullied clouds are blown on a malevolent wind arriving as rain-spats running down the cafe window. Although it is summer it feels like winter and I am marooned alone at The Waves Cafe my heart chained like the surfboard on the wall. There are other customers in the cafe and we all share the warm foody nondescript music atmosphere. However I am isolated by my loneliness, miserably hunched over my coffee that goes cold as I absently stir it.

The music changes and her tune plays "Raspberry beret the kind you buy in a second-hand store." The temperature drops but no door has opened. All activity in the cafe stops as though a freeze frame has been pressed. She appears beside me and as she turns her head towards me I see that her eyes are grey and fathomless like the sea. A halo of droplets surrounds her, clinging to blond hair that hangs like seaweed around her pale lovely face. Her bloodless lips smile as she walks towards the surfboard and I stumble to my feet to follow her. The footprints that she leaves hold no moisture and she disappears as she reaches her goal, leaving me facing the surfboard and the raspberry beret that hangs next to it.

There is a dedication plate also but I have no need to read it as I put it there and the words are carved into my heart, "This surfboard and beret belonged to Jenn known and loved as R.B."

Raspberry Beret lost looking for her big wave – my eyes are red but I cry no more.

The Darkening Season

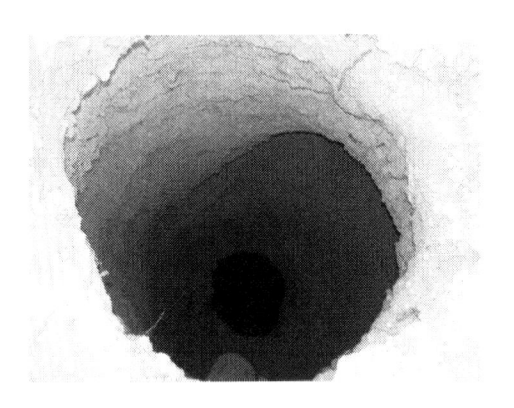

Florida Adventure

Nobody noticed, or rather no humans noticed when a clump of trees disappeared in the swamp. Perhaps a snake or alligator disappeared too but as with the trees there were still plenty left.

The family arrived at the house on the quiet estate they were on holiday, two adults worrying about maxing out their credit cards and two excited children on their first holiday abroad. Their arrival was noticed by two men who looked like garden maintenance workers in a pick-up truck, but Seth and Rick were thieves.

"What do you think Seth are they contenders?" Seth looked at his brother Rick, "Well its quiet enough around here and they have just come from the airport, so they should still have plenty of cash. If its gonna be them it better be tonight before they get spending in Orlando. We'll come back about 1.00am. That will be the sweet spot. They will be nice and sleepy."

"I don't like this house Mum," said Drew the youngest child of the family, "It feels funny."

"Oh for goodness sake, we have only just arrived and you are starting," said his Dad.

The Darkening Season

"But there isn't even a pool," wailed his older sister Haley.

"Well its on a bus route that will take us straight into the resort, we won't be spending much time here and besides it is nice and quiet and clean." Then, under her breath Mum said, "and its cheap!"

Drew would not be placated, he said he could hear funny noises especially in his room.

"Well my bedroom is lovely, I have my own bathroom," said Haley.

Eventually in order to get some sleep the parents gave up their bedroom to Drew and reluctantly decided to sleep on the bedsetee in the lounge, at least for the first night. The bedroom that would have been Drew's was used to house the suitcases and spare bits and pieces of furniture that always seemed to be in the way when you rent a holiday home. Dad also found a neat little lockable cupboard where he could hide the passports, cash and Mum's jewellery.

One o'clock arrived along with Seth and Rick.

"Can you hear a funny slurping noise," whispered Rick. "Na only this noise" Seth replied as he smashed the door of the house in with his boot.

The family were all rounded up and they stared horrified at the ski masked and armed brothers.

"No need for anyone to get harmed," said Seth. "Just hand over the cash and any valuables you have."

"Everything is in the bedroom over there in the little locked cupboard – here's the key," said Dad.

"You had better be telling the truth – Rick go and have a look," said Seth.

As Rick went through the bedroom door three things happened. The lights went out in the house there was a terrible

The Darkening Season

rumbling slurping noise and Rick let out a sickening scream. Forgetting about the family Seth ran into bedroom shouting Rick's name. Dad and Mum took the children's hands and ran through the smashed front door, their escape illuminated by the street lights.

When the Sheriff and deputies arrived they erected wire barriers around the house and yard. No one was going into the house until daylight. After they had been checked over by the paramedics the family were taken to a motel for the night where they huddled together on one of the beds, still in shock.

Next day the house looked just the same as the night before except with the front door hanging where Seth had smashed it in with his boot. At the motel the family had been given tracksuits to wear and were sat in the cafe next to the motel watching TV and eating breakfast. A reporter from the local TV station was interviewing the Sheriff.

"Its a sink-hole" he said and pictures were being shown as a drone flew through the house and went into the bedroom. There was nothing but a gaping hole.

Floor, furniture, suitcases, neat cupboard with the passports cash and jewellery, Rick and Seth, all gone to the same place as the clump of trees and the odd snake and alligator.

The Darkening Season

Tension
(or be careful what you wish for)

Bright lights had been seen in the sky over the town and the residents of Nash Close speculated whether it was UFOs or some secret aircraft flying from the local airbase. It didn't matter what had created this talking point it was a relief to discuss something other than the nightly vandalism and bad doings perpetrated on the Close residents by the neighbours from hell – the Lowe family.

Ma and Pa Lowe and their three teenage sons were always up to something and several families had been driven out of their homes going elsewhere rather than report the Lowes to the police as it would only incur even more grief for themselves if they did. Those who were left lived in a constant state of fear and tension worrying who would be the next target.

One morning, totally unexpected in these circumstances, a sleek small truck arrived at one of the recently vacated houses and out stepped a new family. Mum, Dad and two teenage children a boy and girl. The curtains and blinds of the Close twitched. Fresh victims for the Lowes. How long would they last! The new family seemed a cheerful lot and smiled and waved at their neighbours including Pa Lowe who aimed a twin bogey from his nose at them as he scuttled home to discuss with his lads what new miseries could be concocted.

"Too happy and clean by half," he said. "I think their van needs a-seeing-to and perhaps a dog crap parcel through their letter box for starters."

So it began, a nightly onslaught of foul behaviour. But every morning everything was as it had been.

The van was as sleek as ever with no sign of the gouged paint and the dog crap parcels always ended up in the Lowes front garden, although nobody was seen putting them there. No matter what happened to them the new family carried on smiling and waving.

"I've bloody had enough of this," said Pa. "It ain't natural for nothing to work. I'm going over there tonight to see if I can look in their window and see what they're up to."

The next morning there was something different about the Close. Looking back nobody could remember who was the first to notice that the Lowe family had gone. They had vacated their house all the furniture was gone and the house looked as though it had been scrubbed from top to bottom. The garden that had been a junk-yard was cleared including their several horrible old vans.

A carnival atmosphere pervaded the Close and everyone smile and waved at their neighbours, just like the new family did. In the new family's house everyone was still smiling and showing their lovely white sharp teeth.

Father went to sit in their van on the drive and the neighbours would have been surprised if they had got a look inside as it was huge and full of different banks of equipment and hanging up in storage containers were Ma and Pa Lowe and their three boys. Father opened what looked like a laptop but it was a very powerful transmitter. He pressed keys and the machine sent a

The Darkening Season

series of what sounded like static.

The translation was: FORWARD BASE TO MAIN FORCE – WE ARE EMBEDDED NEAR ONE OF THEIR MILITARY BASES. HAVE SOURCED A LOCAL FOOD SUPPLY. LOOK FORWARD TO YOUR ARRIVAL. THERE IS PLENTY OF FOOD TO GO ROUND. End of message.

The Darkening Season

The Darkening Season

Peter Dawson

Peter is still a Pharmacist. Diversions have included a decade of graduate studies and practice in Canada, a Guardian column on health and social inequalities, endless piano lessons, and ongoing bewilderment with Cosmology. It is now unlikely that he will play football for Manchester Utd.

He is wholly indebted to the Otley Writers Group, without whose friendly support this first effort at fiction would never have happened.

The Darkening Season

Life's Tears

Rain was sleeting down. Daniel's wellingtons sank further into the mud. He was harvesting onions after school, lifting them out of the ground, laying them in wooden trays. He'd carried them into the barn, and was about to spread them out to cure, anxious not to bump or bruise them.

"My eyes on you boy."

Daniel started. The tray crashed to the ground. He rubbed mud from his eyes. He was shaking. "I'm sorry. You frightened me. I didn't know you were there. I'll pick them up."

"Leave 'em be. They're mostly ruined. Get on home to your mother. All the good you've done."

The single light bulb cast shadows. There were other men. Livestock were shifting in the stalls. On the bench he could make out an iron vice, a claw hammer, nails, baler twine, barbed wire.

His father stared uncomprehending, fists clenched. He'd watched the boy struggle in the field. His own boy and such a wuss. She'd made him soft. He was muttering his thoughts out

The Darkening Season

loud. It was a habit. He neither needed nor expected reply. His views weren't up for debate.

"And mind you keep your neb out of my affairs."'.

Reprimands and apologies - surrogates for conversation. Daniel made his escape, ploughing through the mud back to the farm house. He had no desire to meddle in whatever was up in the barn. He had long since been cowed into submission.

Strength, brute strength, was to be admired. That man could scythe three acres a day, and load up corn in hundredweight sacks. He farmed before technology made men soft. Daniel had once seen him punch a cantankerous heifer between the eyes. He was a hard man, like his father. Like father like son. Not always.

"Danny, what have you been up to. You haven't gone upsetting your father again?" His mother read Daniel like a book, and she was tiring of having to take sides. Most nights she would go to bed crying for one or the other, or perhaps for herself.

"I spilt the onions, Mum." His eyes watered as he peeled off the outsized coat and boots and his sodden clothes.

While his mother made him supper, he stood in his underwear, on tip toes reaching deep into the kitchen sink, scrubbing with the hard bristle brush and green soap to get clean. But he knew well enough that no matter how hard he scrubbed, the next day he would still reek of onions, and bear the brunt of classmates' taunts.

He bolted down his supper to get to his bedroom before his father came in. His eyes were still stinging. The lachrymator chemicals are produced to inhibit decay. The most pungent onions are the ones best equipped to survive.

The Darkening Season

The Darkening Season

Pauline Harrowell

I'm a retired civil servant, and I started writing about six years ago; but looking back I think I've always been a word freak and a language geek. For example, I remember as a kid writing a newspaper for my dog.....

Poetry is my default setting, I suppose – but thanks to the encouragement of tutor James Nash and the other members of the Otley Courthouse group I have also tried my hand at short stories and flash fiction. I'm also a member of Saltaire Writers, which is another very supportive environment. Being part of a group is great for your confidence as a writer, and it exposes you to new writing formats (although some of these, such as sonnets and villanelles, are liable to fry your brains). It's thanks to the skills I learned at Otley, and to hours spent staring out of the window muttering, that I managed to get a few poems published. This was a really satisfying achievement.

The Darkening Season

Part Life

Me, I stink of death;
Woe betide you catch my breath -
Rancid reek of dark decay,
Designer stench the zombie way!

Me, I screech and howl,
Bay at the moon, outdo the owl.
Safe at home they block their ears.
Are you the one that wants to hear?

Me, I have soft skin;
The lightest squeeze, you plunge straight in.
Feel it give down to the bone!
I am the sore you can't leave alone.

Me, I drag my chains;
This is how the story ends.
If you believe this to be true
I can't die, and nor can you.

The Darkening Season

The Last Laugh

Gently he takes her hand,
a lover's touch,
her fingers cool and pale as Ophelia's;
the others hold their breath and wait.

The hand that consoled, and wiped away tears,
Scrubbed, cleaned, and tended the stove;
created life and warmth, and helped a friend,
but still knew the moment to recoil,

would never now draw back
from such a love as this.

Gone the perfumed days of youth,
domestic smells of bleach and bathroom,
and now the last austere scent
is pungent and ascetic.

How sweetly skin and flesh part
beneath the scalpel's bloodless kiss;
"And here we see the tendons of the hand..."
He demonstrates how they work;
As her middle finger gave its mocking salute.

The Darkening Season

The Darkening Season

Sandy Wilson

I began writing as a guest contributor of stories for my daughter's blog. These were mainly memoirs of my adolescence in Scotland and of her childhood in Leeds. Then two years ago I joined this extraordinary creative writing group in Otley led by James Nash. Encouraged by James and influenced by the group members I started to explore other genres: fiction, flash fiction and poetry.

My book 'Memory Spill' is a memoir of my childhood in Scotland and my poetry appears in 'Indra's Net', an international anthology of poetry. The profits from Indra's Net support The Book Bus, a charity that provides children's library facilities in Africa, Asia and South America. Both books are available from Amazon.

My flash fiction and short stories have been published on the internet in The Drabble and CafeLit.

I blog as www.sandyscribbler.com

The Darkening Season

Halloween Weekend

From: Sylvia Morgan
To: Francesca Osborne

Re: Halloween Weekend
Tuesday at 9.13

Hi Fran

Do you remember that online competition I told you about, the 1930s Halloween weekend? Well, whoopee! We won it! I couldn't believe it - I've never won anything before in my life! We've been sent train tickets and someone will pick us up and take us to the hotel. The tickets are singles but I expect they'll give us the tickets to get home. We have to dress in 1930s fashion so Bill and I have gone to a fancy dress shop to get kitted out. I've got that lovely Art Deco handbag that belonged to grandma - you remember the one I'm talking about? Anyway, its next weekend and I'll let you know how it goes on.

Sylvia xxxxx

The Darkening Season

Detective Inspector Mike Strasser sat at his desk holding the iPad, the light from the screen reflected off the lenses of his frameless spectacles as he stared at the screen. It had been delivered from Forensic an hour ago and in that time the station I.T. 'geek' Jeb Grant had bypassed the security code.

"That's the first recent email Sir." said Jeb.

"Is there any way to find out where this woman lives?"

"I'll see what I can do. There are some emails from Marks Spencer's and Amazon. I'll contact them."

"Okay, let me know when you find anything else."

"Where was the iPad found Sir?"

"Acklam Hall. I'm off there now."

*

Strasser sketched a salute at the constable standing guard as he drove through the ornate gateway into the building site. It was eerily quiet. Night was falling; the darkening sky descending to the horizon leaving a thin sliver of cold, bright sunlight. The black tracery of bare tree branches and the tendrils of the ivy that cloaked the still standing facade of the ruin almost hid the forbidding maw of the grand entrance doorway and two of the first floor windows; pitch-dark eye sockets that stared at him as he stepped out of his car. Strasser shivered.

The foreman was waiting outside the site office.

"You'll need to wear this," said Mr Ward handing Strasser a yellow hard hat.

They ducked under the blue and white crime scene tape and walked together across to the ruin and climbed the stone stair leading up to the dark doorway. The interior was a dense cats cradle of rotting beams and joists covered with roof slates and stone from the collapsed walls. From the doorway scaffolding and ladders descended through the debris to a cleared space deeper inside the building where floodlights on tripods cast a harsh white light.

"The roof and floors had collapsed into the building. We've been lifting the remains of the beams and joists in layers with the crane," explained Mr Ward. "We found the body under what would have been the ground floor. The TV presenter bloke was the first to see it.. He's pretty shaken."

"TV presenter?"

"Yeah, they're filming the project for one o' them building restoration shows."

"Okay, I'll have a chat with the telly people, then I'll need a statement from you. Where are they?"

"They're over there," said the builder pointing to the trailer bearing the Yorkshire Television logo. "I told them to wait there until you arrived."

As he opened the trailer door he was met by a wall of warm stale air faintly laced with cigar smoke and aftershave. A circle of pale faces looked at him.

"I'm Detective Inspector Strasser. Who's in charge?"

"I am. Phil Proctor. I'm the producer," said a thin, gaunt faced man with a dense ginger beard and red framed designer spectacles. "We're filming an episode of 'Saving the Nation's Architecture'.......This is simply awful. We're all in a tremendous state of shock."

"Yes, I can imagine," said DI Strasser recognising the architect and the historian who fronted the show. "How long have you been filming?"

"Only two days. This is the opening episode," said the producer. "We film at different stages from start to completion of

The Darkening Season

the restoration project. Sometimes over months, even years. We wanted to capture the clearing and preparation of the site."

The inspector explained that everyone must stay in the trailer until interviewed. "I'll start with you, Mr Milner and you, Mr Bartholomew. As the architect and the historian I'd like you both to give me the background of the building. Bit of history and so on. If you would follow me; we'll use the site office."

Strasser's mobile ring tone announced two more emails from Jeb.

From: Francesca Osborne
To: Sylvia Morgan

Re: Halloween Weekend
Tuesday at 10.17

Hi Sylvia

That's brilliant. I hope you have a wonderful time. Do you know how to dance the Charleston?????
Love Fran

From: Sylvia Morgan
To: Francesca Osborne

Re: Halloween Weekend
Yesterday at 4.08

Hi Fran

We arrived this afternoon. When we got off the train a man in a uniform was waiting on the platform, you know like a chauffeur. The car was a vintage model, just like something out of 'Downtown Abbey'. When I said that to the driver he looked puzzled like he was in 'role play'. I think it's really wonderful how they've gone to so much trouble recreating the period. The hotel is very grand - like a stately home. I'll let you know how we get on dancing the Charleston!!
Is it Monday when Jack goes for that interview? Wish him luck from Bill and me.
Love Sylvia

The Darkening Season

In the builder's hut they sat around a trestle table decorated with rings from countless tea mugs and cigarette burns. The air was heavy with the fumes from the Calor gas heater.

Strasser read the emails then said, "I'd like you to give me a bit of the building's history Mr Bartholomew."

"I'd be happy to Detective Inspector." Batholomew said with self importance. "Acklam Hall was designed by Jerome Atkinson in 1833. It's an exceptionally fine example of the neo-classical style with Palladian features. It took four years…."

"I'm more interested in the recent history," said Strasser curtly.

"Oh, I'm sorry!" The historian looked put out. "Well, after the First World War such stately homes were no longer tenable and like so many Acklam Hall was sold by the then owner Bernard Atkinson, the African explorer. In 1927 it became a hotel. Famous for being haunted apparently. Then tragically in 1934 it burned down. It was during a Halloween Ball. After the fire everyone was accounted for, and so the ruins have remained undisturbed since then."

Strasser's mobile vibrated. Another email had been forwarded by the station I.T. geek.

The Darkening Season

> From: Sylvia Morgan
> To: Francesca Osborne
>
> **Re: Halloween Weekend**
> Yesterday at 6.38
>
> Hi Fran
>
> Bill's still upstairs getting ready. It's wonderful just sitting here in the reception watching what's going on. The décor is all black and chrome - Art Deco I think. It's like being on a film set. Even the newspapers are the same date 31 October 1934! The headlines are all about the threat to World peace from Hitler. The trial of the murderer of Charles Lindbergh's son and there's an interesting article about Clark Gable. I thought he won the Oscar for 'Gone with the Wind' but it's for a film called 'It Happened One Night'. There's even a report about a fire in a hotel. That's strange Fran. It's this hotel! Must find Bil.......

Jeb's message ended with: *That's the final email Sir. It just stops mid sentence.*

Strasser thoughtfully put the mobile on the table. "And you Mr Bartholomew, you were first to see the body?"

"I was…. It was horrid. A hand, or actually a badly burned claw protruded from the debris that was being lifted. It was clutching a handbag, sort of Art Deco style. The foreman stopped the crane of course. And then, the strangest thing, the tablet fell out of the bag: an iPad I think. I gave it to the police sergeant who was first to arrive. We were filming at the time so you'll be able to see for yourself…quite awful."

Strasser was about to ask the celebrity architect about the debris removal when he heard the sound of a jazz band coming from the ruin. He opened the hut door and stepped out and walked hesitantly towards the ghostly building with the historian and architect following in his wake. They stopped at the threshold and stared in unified shock. The reception interior was no longer a ruin. The reception was filled with people in evening dress holding champagne glasses and smoking cigars and cigarettes under sparkling chandeliers.

The historian pushed his way through the others and walked to the centre of the throng and looked around in admiration at the ornate wall panelling and the ornate plaster ceiling. The receptionist looked over her desk and smiled as Strasser followed Bartholomew. The music was louder, and the floor vibrated beneath his feet. Through the doorway to his left he could see the black musicians swinging as they played their instruments and dancers moving to the rhythm. Strasser felt light headed.

A woman, sat in a chrome and black leather chair reached up and touched Strasser lightly on the arm. He looked down at her.

"Do you smell burning?" she asked.

The light from the iPad on her lap reflected off the lenses of his frameless spectacles as Strasser stared down at the screen.

*

"Sir…Sir..where was the iPad found?" said Jeb Grant. "Are you okay sir?"

"What?...Sorry. Sorry Jeb..I was somewhere else…..it was found at Acklam Hall. I'm off there now."

The Darkening Season

Nine, Nein? 9!

In November 1986 Ann and I and our daughter Laura are approaching the outskirts of Granada. It is a late holiday to recover from a harrowing year. Ann is in remission; we are optimistic and in good spirits. As we approach the city the snow caps of the Sierra Nevada mountains are draped like clouds in the cloudless blue sky and the Alhambra is touched by the late afternoon sun. It is breathtakingly beautiful.

Before entering the city we stop in a lay-by to review the map. As we ponder the map a man on a moped pulls up alongside us and taps on the window of our Fiat Panda. If we follow him he will lead us into the city, and, of course, he knows of a nice affordable hotel. We shake off the worry that he has the appearance of and might be a bandito and follow him into the beautiful and historic city. Predictably he pulls up in front of the most expensive hotel in Granada, and a concierge in a top hat and a confused expression approaches our battered rental car. As Laura is only nine years old I still my tongue and simply say a polite, "no thank you," in appalling Spanish and drive off leaving the Bandito

The Darkening Season

and the Concierge having a heated conversation in the warm sunlight.

Eventually we find a more suitable, modestly priced establishment: the Hotel Roma. Clean and pleasant, it has an Andalusian style internal central courtyard where we would be served breakfast and the evening meal beside a tinkling fountain. We were lucky to get a room as the hotel was hosting a party of German school children.

One evening we are quietly eating our evening meal as the German children gather noisily around their teacher in the courtyard. The teacher informs the proprietor in English that they are going somewhere cultural and will return at nine o'clock and they file out of the door in Germanic orderly fashion.

Later as we sit at our dining table a phone rings. And rings and rings and rings. The phone is mounted on the wall not far from my head. The proprietor is either profoundly deaf or dead. I'm not. Desperate to stop the racket I decide to answer it. A bad idea.

I impersonate a receptionist "Hallo, this is the Hotel Roma." The line is poor and the line fizzles and crackles.

"Gut, gut, I vish to speak with my son Hans." Says the caller. "Is 'e zer?"

Through the hissing and crackling I pick up the German accent and just catch the name Hans. Obviously Hans is one of the school kids.

"He is not here. He will be back at nine." I carefully explain in the pedantic way we British speak to foreigners.

"Vot! Hans, 'e is not there?" says the anxious voice.

"Nine. He will be back at NINE!" I repeat impatiently

"Nein?"

"Yes, NINE."

The Darkening Season

But through the crackling of the phone line the concerned father is probably only hearing the word nine, or in his case: nein, German for no.

"You say NO!, Hans, 'e is not at the hotel! Ver can 'e be!"
"No, I said NINE!"
"Nein?"
"NINE!"
"NEIN?"

This verbal tennis match with the word 'nine' continues for a few moments more, then, hearing the proprietor coming through from the kitchen, I hang the handset back on the cradle terminating the call. As the coffee is poured into the white china cups I say nothing. It was just too surreal.

As I quietly sip my café con leche I have a mental picture of a German Vater in Düsseldorf or Hamburg sat staring at his telephone in anxious disbelief.

The Darkening Season

Beautiful Dance of Death

The sun, a pale orb, looks down
as chill winds careen and caper
through the tracery of branches.
Thrumming timeless hymns
Nature's long forgotten songs

Perching on swaying boughs
funereal crows in mourning clothes
flap wings black and feathery.
Trapeze artistes seeking balance
as they cry their discordant chorus

Leaves lose their tenuous grip
Fall, cascading to the ground
to join the multicoloured cavalcade.
Prancing harlequins dancing
across slick grass and damp slab

I stand silent, listen and watch
this wintry, beautiful dance of death

The Darkening Season

The Witch Who Fell To Earth

Lily hated where she lived. Even though they had only moved in three months ago lots of awful things had happened. It was a very unlucky house she thought. An unhappy house.

Only last week when she arrived home Lily had passed a small round man as he emerged from the front door. He smiled at her as he bounced down the steps and walked past her.

"Who was that?" She asked her mum who was holding the door open for her.

"Mr Jones, the Neighbourhood Watch Coordinator. Somebody's broken into the garage again. I'm sorry Lil, they stole your bike, Charlie's too. Mr Jones called round to give me advice about security; make sure we lock doors, fit alarms; things like that. He's a kind and helpful man."

Lily had loved her bicycle and felt sad.

Then this morning as she was getting ready to go to school, pulling her coat on in the hallway, she found another horrid letter.

This time it said: GO HOME TO AFRICA WHERE YOU BELONG in letters cut from a magazine or a newspaper. She took the letter to show her mother and said. "But mum, I was born here so I must belong here!" Her mum, remembering Eritrea where she 'belonged', cried.

"We should move, mum. Live somewhere else." Lily had said as she hugged her mother. "I hate this house!"

Later, in the afternoon, as Lily sat at her desk in the classroom, worry-worms slithering around in her head, she heard the teacher clap her hands and say, "Now, children it's time to get ready for the concert!"

With her worrying Lily had forgotten that there was the Halloween concert that afternoon. The children dressed up in their witch's costumes and applied face paint, laughing and giggling at how scary they looked. Then the excited children walked across the playground to the assembly hall to sing as a chorus in the Halloween concert.

Lily had been walking in deep thought at the back of the noisy straggling line when with a WHOOMP! a real witch had stumbled into her in a cloud of peculiar sparkling dust, flying twigs and a smell that reminded Lily of biscuits or burnt toast. It was as though this odd person had fallen from the sky: which she had.

The witch gripped Lily's arm with her long bony fingers. "Please, please, help me," she said in a strange hissing voice. "I am Jezebel."

She was nearly as tall as Lily with wild hair under a black conical hat and a hook nose. In her hand she held the remnants of a broom.

Lily, although surprised and frightened, considered this strange person extremely polite. Her mum and dad had taught her to help people, especially when they were polite. She took Jezebel's hand, smiled to reassure her and hurried to catch up with

The Darkening Season

her classmates who were too excited to notice the witch. Lily decided to help her now and ask questions later.

As they walked through the door of the assembly hall, the music teacher Miss Baldwin strode towards Lily and the cluster of small witches.

"Now children I want you to stand by the piano....."

She paused as she looked down at the upturned faces. The face paint made them look like witches but one looked surprisingly realistic.

"And who are you?" she said to the unfamiliar face.

"Her name is Jezebel, Miss," said Lily.

"Jezebel?" Miss Baldwin repeated the strange name.

Lily improvised, "Yes, Miss. Jez is in class four. She's new to the school."

Miss Baldwin was quiet for a worrying moment. But, she was only considering the odd names parents can give their children. And, she thought, it wasn't just pop stars and celebrity chefs that dreamt up fantastic names for their offspring. There was a boy called Zeus with the Mohican hair cut in class six and there had been a girl called Moon at her last school.

"Well, um..Jez..go with Lily and stand with rest of the girls," she said.

Lily sighed with relief. Saying a lie about Jez was a great worry as real witches were not nice. In fact she had read lots of scary witch stories.

The concert was a great success although Lily though Jez was not a great singer. She had made a low pitched keening sound which Miss Baldwin didn't appear to notice.

At the end of the concert when the enthusiastic applause died down, the proud parents left the hall with their children to go home.

The Darkening Season

"Where are your mother and father?" hissed Jezebel.

"Don't worry, they're not here. They're both at work." explained Lily. "You'd better come home with me."

As they left the assembly hall to walk across the playground to the school gates Lily and Jez passed the head mistress Mrs Cunningham and the school caretaker Sam. They were standing around the strange scorch marks in the playground and the scattering of twigs, looking puzzled.

When they reached Lily's home her grandfather opened the front door.

"Hello Lil. How did the concert go?"

"It was great Gramps. Miss Baldwin was pleased. She said everyone sang well."

"This a friend of yours?" he said looking down at Jez.

"Yes. This is Jez, Gramps. She's a real witch!" said Lily.

"Don't tell mum and dad!"

"I won't Lil. Mum's the word, eh?" Tapping the side of his nose as Lily led Jez past him into the hall and down into the basement.

"You must hide down here Jez."

"Hide me? Why not tell your parents?" Jezebel hissed.

"Well, you're a witch!"

"What's wrong with being a witch?"

"People think witches aren't nice." said Lily, adding, "I'm sure you're okay, but there's lots of stories about things witches do. They're always casting spells: turning people into frogs, that sort of thing!"

"Pish! You shouldn't trust everything you read," rasped Jezebel. "I've turned no one into a frog…….well, there was someone… but not for long."

The Darkening Season

"Well, there you are. You'll have to stay down here for a bit."

"But you told that old man I'm a witch."

"Oh, that's just Gramps. He's my grandfather, and he forgets things. He won't remember you."

Lily cleared a space in the corner under the stairs and built a wall around an old mattress using empty suitcases and removal boxes.

"It looked cosy," she thought.

"Stay here. I've got to help Gramps make dinner for when mum and dad come home," said Lily. "I'll bring food for you later."

"I don't need food," hissed Jezebel.

"But you need to eat. Everyone does!"

"I do not eat food I live off the air."

"Yeah, right. Suit yourself, but keep very quiet."

While Lily went upstairs to the kitchen Jezebel sat cross legged on the mattress and emptied the deep pockets of her black cloak. There was a small sphere she could cup in her hands which looked as if was full of swirling fog with tiny lights that sparkled. She placed the sphere in front of her on the mattress. Then she pulled out a bunch of willow twigs and arranged them around the sphere in the shape of a star. Satisfied that the sphere and the twigs were arranged correctly she sat still and closed her eyes.

Later, after dinner Lily brought her little brother Charlie to meet the witch. She felt she had to share her secret with someone. They both looked into the den Lily had made.

"Hi Jez. This is my brother Charlie," said Lily.

Charlie looked but couldn't see anybody. This didn't surprise him. Only last week Lily claimed to have three dinosaurs in the back of the car when their dad took them swimming and another time she had an invisible friend called Florence. His sister could be really annoying sometimes.

"He cannot see me. I have cast a spell. I am invisible to everyone but you."

"Well, you must undo the spell otherwise he'll think I'm lying."

To Charlie's astonishment Jez shimmeringly took shape.

"There. I told you!" said Lily. "She's a real witch; a nice one of course!"

"Hey! That's so wicked!" exclaimed Charlie.

"What does he mean 'wicked'?" hissed the witch wondering if she might just change this horrible boy into a toad or an earwig.

"No, Jez. He means 'cool' you know, like amazing."

Jezebel looked at Charlie with narrowed eyes and decided not to turn him into a toad then hissed, "You have a stream of negative energy running through your house."

She explained that it was like having a chill wind blowing through the house, a wind that brought bad luck.

"That doesn't surprise me!" said Lily.

"How do you know?" said Charlie. "I can't see anyone!"

"I will show you." rasped Jez as she reached into a pocket and pulled a pair of twigs bent in the shape of the letter L. Holding a twig in each hand she walked across the basement. Suddenly the twigs swivelled towards each other.

"It flows through here!"

"You could be moving the twigs yourself," Charlie said.

Jezebel narrowed her eyes. "Listen, you horrible little boy. I could turn you into a..a..snail! You'd like that, eh!" She hissed handing Charlie the twigs. "Here try it yourself if you don't trust me."

The Darkening Season

Charlie held the twigs in his hands and walked across the room. To his surprise the twigs moved in his hands in precisely the same place. "You're right," he whispered. "Can you get rid of it?"

"Oh yes. I can make it go somewhere else."

Jezebel searched through her deep pockets and brought out a handful of crystals like brightly coloured glass: red as blood, green as holly leaves and blue as a summer sky. She told the children that they must bury the crystals in the north west corner of your garden. Lily and Charlie followed Jez through the door and up the moss covered steps to the garden. An app. on Charlie's mobile showed where the north west corner was, then in the light of the street lamps they swept away the dead leaves and dug a hole in the damp soil. Jezebel, muttering a spell in her rasping voice dropped the crystals in the hole and the children covered them with soil and replaced the leaves.

Back in the basement Jezebel and the children sat cross legged on the mattress.

"Close your eyes." hissed Jezebel. "Listen."

Their home let out a long sigh. They could hear the old timbers creaking and stretching and the stones and bricks settling as their home relaxed.

"There, can you feel it? Sense the happiness return?" Jezebel hissed. "The stream of misfortune has gone."

"Where's it gone?" asked Lily and Charlie.

At 54 Burton Grove, the bungalow on the other side of the road, the doors and windows rattled, the lights flickered and the net curtains fluttered. In the kitchen old Peter Jones muttered in annoyance as the strange draught blew across the table scattering the letters he had just cut out of the morning's newspaper and last week's copy of his wife's 'Woman's Weekly' ready to glue on the sheet of paper in front of him. As he bent down to pick up the

The Darkening Season

scattered scraps of paper from the floor, he felt a strange sense of foreboding.

The Darkening Season

Don't be late

When I waited in spring
Under the cherry tree
As the blossom fell
Like confetti
You were late

When I waited in summer
Under the cherry tree
As the green leaves
Shaded me
You were late

Then I waited in Autumn
Under the cherry tree
As leaves fell dead
To the ground
You were late

Now, I wait in winter
Under the cherry tree
As snow flakes fall
In the cold air
Don't be late, again

Just fucking don't

The Darkening Season

OTLEY WRITERS PUBLICATIONS

Writers write to be read, or what is the purpose of it all? This sounds like something I may have read somewhere, but it is what I truly believe. This innate need to be read led our creative writing group Otley Writers to publish our own works.

'The Darkening Season', our second anthology is an exciting collection of fiction, memoir and poems. And, astonishingly for such a small group, many members too have published their own books in a wide range of genres from crime fiction to horror and children's stories to memoir. Information about these exciting publications can be found on the next few pages.

The Darkening Season

'The Body in Jingling Pot' is a murder mystery that introduces Detective Chief Inspector Oldroyd. A local man is found murdered in a cave system in strange circumstances. The case proves to be a perplexing investigation for Jim Oldroyd with no shortage of suspects. Set in the Yorkshire Dales the book reflects author John Ellis's love of the region and Yorkshire culture.

'The Quartet Murders' is the second Chief Inspector Oldroyd murder mystery. It is set in Halifax in Yorkshire where a violin player is murdered during a performance attended by Jim Oldroyd. The resulting criminal investigation involves a priceless violin, the ruthless world of wealthy instrument collectors and the theft of valuable artefacts by the Nazis during the Second World War.

'Memory Spill' by Sandy Wilson is a humourous and at times poignant account of his childhood in Scotland. The memoir begins in 1953 and spans almost two decades. It is a time when life was uncomplicated. At Lasswade Primary School an inappropriate film is screened, a railway station mysterious burns down and children dance with the devil...........

The Darkening Season

'Badlands' by Alyson Faye is a collection of flash fiction pieces, from drabbles of 100 words to longer pieces up to 1000 words. Written over the last three years my short shorts reflect my interest in ghost stories, history, old movies, real life issues such as homelessness and just the 'what if' factor when a seemingly normal situation starts to tilt off centre, leading to dangerous waters.

'The Runaway Umbrella' is a book with illustrations for children aged 7-10 years. Izzy buys a penguin umbrella from the Rainy Days shop. When a wind gets up the umbrella takes flight. Izzy sets off on a chase helped by various people, but there is something magical about it. Will she ever catch it?

'Soldiers in the Mist' by Alyson Faye is a book for children aged 13 – 14. It is set in Norwich and on the Norfolk Broads. It is a time-slip adventure story scattered with clues. Sara and her brother are in a dangerous race against the evil Smythes to solve the mystery of the lost Roman gold and the fate of the Roman soldiers.

The Darkening Season

Before the Second World War there were around seventy cinemas operating in Leeds. Now, though some remain open, most of these 'forgotten temples' have been repurposed or demolished. Since 2014 Leeds-based poets James Nash and Matthew Hedley Stoppard have produced an evocative poetry collection celebrating these legendary picture houses with two inimitable, un mistakable poetic voices.

Maggie Moore's hilarious adventures over one school year. She gets the worst part in the schoolplay, her world record attempt goes disastrously wrong and as for her act in the talent show, well let's just say she didn't expect underpants to fly out of her trumpet and land on the judge's face. Still at least she has three best friends and this, her diary.
Alex L Williams writes as Firna Rex Shaw.

Meet Eric Trum, the stick man with a big bum. This is another children's character from the inventive mind of Alex L Williams writing as Jonny Staples. Find out how things don't always run smoothly for the little stick man. If it's not his large bottom getting in the way, its his neighbour Jeremy Mothballs, trying to spoil his fun. How will he cope?

The Darkening Season

Chris Moran's poetry is eclectic and entertaining, even whimsical, spiritual and philosophical, deeply personal and relatable. The book charts her recovery from alcoholism and the depths of despair and subsequent multiple sclerosis diagnosis. Her poetry documents her life with courageous honesty and unexpected humour. Profits from this book go to the Multiple Sclerosis Trust.

With these endlessly inventive and marvellous poems Glenda Kerney Brown explores the things that she values, the things she cleaves to, and the underlying tragedy of our human experience, which is that we inevitably lose the things we love. With an artist's palette Glenda commemorates the past, celebrates the present and contemplates the future in honest and beautiful poetry.

Writers from all over the world generously donated their poetry for inclusion in this international anthology in aid of The Book Bus Charity. The Book Bus aims to improve child literacy in Africa, Asia and South America by providing children with books and the inspiration to read them.
Otley Writers included in this anthology are:
Glenda Kerney Brown, Alyson Faye, Chris Moran and Sandy Wilson.

The Darkening Season

CHEVIN
Manuscripts

Acknowledgments

Andy Driver of AddCreative designed the book cover. Andy is a graphic artist and website designer. www.addcreative.co.uk

Kevin Hickson provided the backround photographic image. Kevin is a Leeds based artis

Alyson Faye and **John Ellis** edited and proof read the book.

Sandy Wilson designed and set out the book interior

Printed in Great Britain
by Amazon